WRITTEN MUSIC
IDEATION

Its European Story

Michael G. Cunningham

AuthorHouse™
1663 Liberty Drive
Bloomington, IN 47403
www.authorhouse.com
Phone: 1 (800) 839-8640

Published by AuthorHouse 06/03/2015

ISBN: 978-1-4969-5876-1 (sc)
ISBN: 978-1-4969-5877-8 (e)

Table of Contents

Written Music Ideation
(Its European story)

First: Finding a way of writing it down. Later: Attempts at quality, and an overview of Instruction in its methods.

by **Michael G. Cunningham**, with help from many sources.

Chapter 1   INTRODUCTION

MUSIC IDEATION

In prehistoric primitive times we can assume that early man found it stimulating and functional to sound out rhythms on drums. What follows here will not deal with that continuing universal tendency. Instead, we will deal with pitch-oriented sounds. First we will trace progress towards finding a way of notating music. Then, in a cursory manner, we will trace the growth of notation, and following that, citations of attempts to write quality ideation with sets of rules.

Back at the beginnings of civilization, musically endowed individuals first mentally experienced the melodic idea, after which it was brought to life acoustically. Often these two stages were simultaneous. This process has perhaps been timeless. These heard sounds, perhaps improvised, and at first attached (sung) to verbal expression, were performed, eventually aided with musical instruments that were at hand. This we later identify as music. It was easy for words to be sung to music, and even to be confused with music. Back in the earliest days, the difference between musical ideation and text/poetry was blurred, and both were wrongly thought a single medium. However, if need be, music would always be able to stand on its own without words. But with its separation from texts, just what is music? After advances in literacy and human thought were later achieved, that question that would crop up occasionally over the following millennia would involve whether it was the product of scientific factors, or of humanistic phenomenon. For now we will temporarily postpone that issue. Instead, let us continue thinking about those earliest appearances of music.

Let us assume that civilized man wanted to repeat musical experiences that were deemed worth saving. (We can also assume that esthetic reactions helped dictate what was worth saving.) Over time, any attempts to repeat ingrained music were reliant on the memories of the performers. But memories were inexact and tended to change the original ideation. Ironically, that kind of change in itself would prove eminently typical of music, and would later be known as variation. However, in the earliest days there arose a need to record in some sort of written symbols the original ideation so as to freeze in time as much of the original music as was possible. This was especially important when it came to sacred music. Hence, the musical ideation came first, then after a way was found, the writing of it into symbols that others in later generations, could read and reproduce. This necessitated training programs. If we consider early civilizations, it would be a fair estimate that it took thousands of years from the first appearance of improvised melodies, seemingly fused with text, for mankind to develop a notation of them.

The late Classic Greek culture that prevailed in the post-Alexander Hellenistic empire fostered a musical notation that, except for a few written comments, remains mostly unknown to us. Perhaps had the library at Alexandria not burned in 47 B.C.E. we might know more, but alas, that was not to be. The few surviving late Classical Greek prose writings are complicated, and are made further so by the dwelling on needlessly complex terms and concepts. Moreover, those terms and concepts had gradually changed during the Hellenistic centuries. (More on that later.) What little the Greeks wrote survived in the succeeding Roman period, and still later in monasteries, where they were valued and studied. Ironically, the relative security prevalent during the Roman hegemony resulted in little, if any progress in writing about music, and there was nothing on notation. However, the Romans can be thanked for passively allowing Greek culture to survive. Through it all, we can assume that the

Romans always experienced a non-literate functional and ceremonial music, the kinds of which we can only guess.

As Rome was falling, there was a slow progress towards written music, aided by the needs of the Christian Church. In time the Christians would value music. Compounding the slow progress towards literacy after Rome's collapse, and during the intervening Middle Ages, there were wars and plagues that indeed slowed the development of civilization in general. Still, with its preservation, the bulk of Hellenistic writings would prove of some use to the later growth of European music and its eventual literacy. It is true that Hellenistic scale/modes were influential, but almost by accident and by misunderstanding. Therefore, the Western Europeans were mostly "on their own" in the inevitable growth of Occidental music. Also, a Hellenistic crude form of notation proved practically useless. The few examples that survived were on stone and remained lost for a couple thousand years. Moreover, the examples involve only melody, and ultimately were a dead-end issue.

THE WORD THEORY:
Here we will temporarily pause in our time-line of history by citing chosen points in time. Moving into the early Christian or Common Era, as Roman law and order was slowly eroding (300s-500s), the concept of Music Theory came about. Maybe the contemplation of music, and notions of attachment with science came from the Greeks. The adoption of such a pompous-sounding label, whether in the 500s or later, would in time seem to weigh down the delicate butterfly wings of Music. To the medieval mind, the word Theory seems to have meant the writing about, and reflecting on music rather than its performance. But to that mind, this abstraction could involve far more. Later Medieval writings could easily saddle music with the motion of the stars and planets, Eternity and other far-flung associations. (Again, no doubt brought about by esthetic reactions to the music.) And there were historic figures who just stayed fixated on tunings and mathematics. This would always be an ongoing and heavy departure from the rather simple needs of how to create music, and possible ways to write it down.

Roman citizen Anicius Boethius, writing in the early 500s C.E. translated and transmitted Hellenistic music writings, muddled and complex as they were, to the Latin world, and hence to the following modern era. Later Medieval musicians subsequently relied heavily on Boethius. We can read him today in translations, and in so doing we find that he transmits nothing about written notation.

After Boethius, progress certainly slowed while all of European civilization endured seemingly endless and unchecked roving pillagers and marauders. No wonder stone fortresses were typical of Medieval times. After several centuries of turbulent mayhem it is amazing that any culture survived, let alone any writings about music. (More about that survival will be discussed later.) It seemed that, since the first century C. E., there had always been monks sequestered away in monasteries that were often in remote locations. Their multiple activities also involved preserving culture. Often the monks were the only literate individuals to found, and often the monks were more literate than the ruling classes. The monks thus had an unintended monopoly on culture. They recopied aging, rotting manuscripts, and thus had access to articulate thought that had been hand-written on the sparse writing surfaces that had earlier existed. (Often that surface was animal-skin/parchment.) Such writings would seem to the early monks, and even to we moderns, to be cryptic and sometimes philosophical. ("Theory") The writings could also involve Ancient Greek tunings, and thus seeming proof for some that music was indeed the result of naturalistic overtone relationships, and ultimately of mathematical calculations.

The chanting of monophonic hymns had seemingly always been part of the Christian liturgy, and where it came from remains up for debate. (Did it come from Western tradition, the Eastern Church? Constantinople?) There were efforts by the early Western (Roman) Churchmen to organize the existing music, and they did so without benefit of a written notation. That organization evidently took place in the 500s and 600s. By the 800s the monks and clergy were building on the Greek writings so as to move towards tonal literacy. Developments were taking place that helped bring about notation. One could even say that it became necessary because of singers simultaneously performing different "remembered" versions of any given melody. Definitive written versions became increasingly important.

In the succeeding Medieval centuries the pompous concept and title "Theory" continued, and official music went on being weighed down with their notions of science and philosophy. It may have been that prose writers were so moved by the liturgical music that they concluded it simply had to be connected with Metaphysics and Eternity. (Ironically modern specialists in Esthetics touch upon such human reactions when they try to define Esthetics and Beauty.) When given as a subject in the newly emerging Medieval universities, Music Theory was equated with the other sciences of the day. The concept of Music Theory in all its pretensions would undergo some changes in the following Renaissance and well into the following centuries, when metaphysical associations were downplayed or outright dropped.

Perhaps "Theory's" most interesting overtone-measurement phase was in the Baroque period when Jean-Philippe Rameau sprang his pseudo-scientific overtone findings on the Paris Intellectual establishment. By then, Theory was concerned mainly with Harmony. But still, one wonders if the label Theory really is appropriate? Getting musical ideation down on paper was the first, and probably the only process that mattered in the long run, and side excursions into non-musical thought, and maybe even overtone "coincidences" should be regarded as long-term and ultimately temporary digressions. Certainly Rameau was on to something, but it was not enough proof that music was a rational Science, a proof that his middle 1700s ardent contemporaries were wishing for. And why just Harmony? Musicians of all historic periods would never need, or plead for instruction in melodic construction or in rhythm. Those areas were too easily grasped or individualized. It was Harmony, in its broadest sense, which would foster Theoretical writings and instruction. (More on Rameau later.)

As mentioned earlier, the first appearance of notation was made necessary because of the need to record simultaneously differing melodies or lines. Then later, what propelled the need for yet more specific musical explanations was the emergence of triadic harmony in the 1400s. The later Baroque period had music with almost equal attention to the outer voices, melody and bass. Harmonic progressions were the typical. J. Sebastian Bach taught Theory that involved harmony in the form of figured basses. By Mozart and Beethoven's time notions of Theory had nestled into mere note-movement procedures involving counterpoint fitting into harmony. By the 20th and 21st Centuries a new definition of Theory seemed to have become official. It said that Theory study concerns itself mainly with the construction of Music. While logicians might ask the question, "Where did such and such a sound come from in nature?", musicians would prefer to ignore that question. Instead, musical thinkers and composers would concern themselves with established sounds fitting into a proper context. It would be comforting to many to define Theory as the mental reasoning behind composition. However, maybe the word Theory, even with such a definition, has come to mean too much.

As a field of study today, Music Theory in the 20th and 21st centuries could also involve any writings that attempt to explain the phenomenon of music. Any attempt to sidestep the notion of endowed individuals creating inexplicable phenomena intuitively would be welcome. The prevailing hope seems was/is that transferrable logic has to be involved. There should be concrete, provable reasoning. The staples of modern Theory are presently seen as Harmony, Melody and Rhythm. Additionally, highly specialized areas might involve Pitches, Tuning and Temperaments, Intervals, Consonance/Dissonance, Scales/Modes, Meter, Duration, Timbre, collections of sounds, Acoustics, Form, Analysis, new or novel approaches to the three staples, and World Music Cultures. This is Theory with an extended reach indeed. Yet, what is more elusive is the esthetic "high" a listener experiences while hearing a great symphony: the passage of feeling. That idea, of course, reopens the issue the Medieval writers had touched upon: music and Eternity.

Yet, further areas for Theory specialization involve music as related to Science, Acoustical measurements and Mathematics. Areas of physical phenomenon might involve studies in the Overtone Series and derivations such as calculations of proportions, chords and scales, interval ratios, Hertz ranges, odd overtones from diversely shaped objects, timbre calculations involving formants, and Fourier Mathematics that calculate overtones. Studies might involve the infamous Pythagorean Comma, Just/Natural Intonation, piano voicing, the "Wolf" and sympathetic vibration. An added concomitant is that the writings on these various topics might be cloaked in abstruse language, thus giving credence to the warning, "If people don't understand what you are saying, they won't know what you are saying wrong."

However, this book deals with the writing of music, and of actual headway made in the evolution of written music leading to the music of our present time. Moreover, very little space is devoted here to writers who had unique ideas that ultimately went nowhere. There were plenty of false detours and eccentric indulgencies, often the work of sincere authors and innovators who usually had admirable intentions, and who often attracted some followers. The question should always be whether any explanation of the mechanics of music led to actual scores that survived, scores that were respected by succeeding generations of musicians. (By the Twenty-first Century certain libraries seemed to be well-stocked with singular research on musical activities and speculations that went nowhere.) Here we are concerned with techniques that are maintained over a long stretches of time; techniques that grow or transform; and sometimes involving thought and approaches that are rediscovered after an earlier neglect.

In telling this story it is impossible to avoid naming some of the greatest composers of various periods, and so their names will appear. When it comes down to actual pieces of music, the Darwinian notion of "survival of the fittest" has remained true throughout history. Maybe there have always been well-meaning revisionists who sift through obscure music, and seemingly hope to revise history, so that all old music is equivalent. Even as the 21st Century progresses, there seems to be an attempt to commercially record all old music, and indeed to play it over the radio. While at first that can seem a good thing, in reality quality music, as well as those capable of judging it, become lost if not disoriented amid the morass. If a previously unknown composer or piece of music is discovered and shown to be great, so much the better. However, that is usually not the case. We should trust the taste of former generations of musicians. If enough of them felt that a certain composer or his music was valuable, indeed it was and remains.

In today's university, those who administer and plan music degrees, and those who teach Music Theory cannot seem to agree as to what Theory is, and why it should be in the curriculum. Amid some disagreement, there seems to be an unspoken agreement that Theory instruction helps students become literate in the language of music notation. In blunt terms, they should be able to play on an instrument, or sing the notation they see. And they should use notation to write somewhat creatively, and they should hear music to the point of being somewhat able to write it down. This is often described as Basic Musicianship. However, as musicians' skills develop, what is the next goal after that? Some feel that it is to enable the student to compose the latest fashionable style. "Take Theory so you'll be able to write music to suit your own notion of what music is, and maybe it will be commercially viable." The goal is therefore seen as vocational training in immediate marketable skills. With that kind of thinking there is no historic past or future to consider. Music only exists in the present, and what is written should probably just be cast aside in the fullness of time because it will no longer be relevant. However narrow, that goal is not all bad, and could be amended and seen as a side benefit to Theory instruction. Others feel that the study of Theory should enable the student to talk intelligently about music. Here music is regarded as insufficient because it is non-verbal, and it somehow gains validity when it is transferred into the world of words. However narrow, that goal could also only be an additional side benefit.

The highest goal for students is to understand great music literature created by great minds. Theory instruction helps to understand the procedures and mind-set that went into those great works. Traditional "Tonality" Theory, like it or not, should have as its goal a better understanding of the inner mechanics of concert/recital music, bulk of which was written between 1700 and 1900. Newly created Theoretical courses can be devised so as to deal with the music of the succeeding century. Theory is thus not studies in Composition, though Composition skill could be a side benefit if one accepts the notion that truly creative minds will select, transfer and adapt seemingly topic-specific information to a style quite different from what is actually being studied.

Chapter 2 THE ANCIENT GREEKS AND THEIR WRITINGS

If one takes the year when the Athenians established democracy, and extends it to the year of Alexander's death, the period of high Classicism lasted only about 190 years. Speculative writings on music were begun during that period and were to continue during the so-called Hellenistic period following Alexander's death. Thus ancient Greek Theory existed and evolved over five or more centuries, and was anything but constant, consistent, unified or simple. Different writers said differing things. Modern scholars are often careful not to become too enmeshed in its complexities. One suspects that much of what the writers said was too individualistic, and would prove useless to further growth in the coming A.D. or Common Era (C.E.). Today it would all be so much simpler if we could only hear the musical examples described in the Ancient abstruse writings. Still a number of points came through the fog that would prove to be useful in the coming millennia.

HOW MUCH OF MUSIC IS SCIENTIFIC and HOW MUCH IS EMPIRICAL AND TASTE?
The monochord with its single string proved useful to the ancient Greeks. Some twenty years before the first vote on democracy, the monochord enabled Pythagoras to experiment with, and to establish certain truisms involving "harmonics," various intervals and string proportions. (We have Euclid to thank for transmitting Pythagoras' thoughts some 120 years after their initial proclamation.) Pythagoras believed that music and mathematics were one. Is that so? Music that is explained in such a mathematical a way remains an ongoing issue even in modern times. It is likely that all through Greek Classical history most practicing musicians disagreed with the premise. Using intervals, it was possible for Pythagoras to construct a complete diatonic scale by a series of alternating perfect 4th and 5th tunings. And when he reached the octave, that note would be sharp. That discovery involving the distance the octave note should be and the actual arrival note is called the Pythagorean Comma. We can duplicate Pythagorean tunings with tests on a stretched string. When it comes to tunings, his findings are clear and inarguably valid.

There were other Greek practices that proved viable in the later Christian era. After about 200 years of various and conflicting musical systems, Aristoxenus and Cleonides, contemporaries of Alexander, help to clarify much about Greek tetrachord Theory. Also, the writings of so-called Ptolemy (Ptolemais, a woman?), to be explained later, were of help then and now. And, as indicated earlier, there was Boethius, a late Roman translator/copyist. Working around 510 C.E. , he is our connection to the early Greeks of some 800 years earlier. His writings would enable Medieval theorists to construct their own system that in turn grew into Renaissance and Baroque musical reasoning. Accepting Boethius' sometime flawed translations, the later Medieval writers thought they were faithfully reconstructing what the Ancient Greeks had established. Boethius, in his translation, confused the direction successive Greek modes, and pitches, moved from a point of reference. He assumed that the Greeks were labeling successive scalar modes upward, when the Greeks were really reasoning downward. But in spite of that error, we can still, in a general way, relate the Christian Era modes to those of the Greeks. We can also posit that in both eras hyper/hypo and plagal modes were really a way of dealing with inherently lower voice ranges (altos and basses). We can also relate their four-note units (tetrachords) to our modern scales. Their enharmonically shaded tetrachords, with their impossibly far-fetched numerical justifications, even served a roundabout purpose in later times. These seemingly far-fetched tunings probably resulted in forms of what we would later call pentatonicism. But the parallels with later European music only go so far. Much of the Greek reasoning remains impenetrable, and, if understandable, then useless in terms of the later growth of Occidental music.

ANCIENT GREEK COMPLEXITY
From Grecian Democracy's beginning, and for 150 years – up to the time of Plato, Greek Theory became more and more complex. Their nomenclature (name designation) for every item or detail they discuss is uniquely multi-syllabic, and that would remain so until time of the Christian era medieval innovators. For instance, whereas we would say D – F – G – A, they would assign long multisyllabic names for each of those scale degrees. This feature certainly adds to the complexities of

their writings. Then after Plato's time (around 380 BCE), a reaction set in against some of the complexity, and gradually with the writings of Aristoxenus and Cleonides, and over the next two centuries the whole process was simplified, and no doubt standardized. It is from this period that we get clearer explanations of their four-note groupings, their shadings, as well as other information. Aristoxenos and Eratocles speak of a complete chromatic scale, still with a unique word label for each note. They also describe a thirteen key system that accommodated their scalar/modal system. The Theorist Ptolemy (or possibly a woman, Ptolemais) was an pseudononymous writer who flattered the then Greek Pharaoh by using the ruler's dynastic name. That person, writing in Alexandria during the pre-Roman period, is very helpful in describing Greek scalar tuning complexities and a growing standardization of octave scales.   This writer also believed that both intuition and mathematics were necessary for music. But at other times the writing just meanders off into specific practices and complexities that would not survive in Occidental music in the coming Christian Era.

Poetry and music were inseparable to the Greeks. In all likelihood the sung rhythm merely matched the textual needs. Undoubtedly metric rhythm did exist, because of the universality of steady beats and the natural tendency to make strong and weak beats. However, there are no surviving writings concerning meter. To Ancient Greeks the chosen scale-type, rhythm and the motivic activity all affected the ethos of the music, and a particular ethos could supposedly change one's behavior for the good or bad. Scale formation was naturally important, and along with each scale a particular behavior was attached. To the Greeks, when making music, as opposed to mere abstract description, it was tetrachord (four note) units that really mattered.   To them, notes an octave apart had different multi-syllabic labels. In one case there were even different names for notes that are two octaves apart. Imagine our pitch A in three octaves with a different name for each. On the other hand, their interval labels seem more logical to the modern reader.

The music described is monophonic. The Tetrachords usually came in three types, or shadings called Genera: Diatonic, Chromatic and Enharmonic. Each type would fill in the notes of a Perfect 4th, the framing notes being unchangeable. Stacked tetrachords were used to tune the strings of the limited range Lyre, or the eleven-string Kithara. Tuning of their instruments was constantly changeable in order to accommodate chosen scale constructs. The Kithara was actually just a larger Lyre, and was used by the more professional performers. Of the two instruments, the Kithara in particular, enabled clearer Theoretical/systematic scalar thinking. These stringed instruments were felt akin to the god Apollo, who symbolized thoughtful contemplation. Thus Apollo was an appropriate "overseer" for speculative Theory.

THE "BOETHIUS MISTAKE"
Whereas modern musicians have always thought upwards in creating scales and labeling scale degrees, the Ancient Greeks always thought downward from a point-of-reference.   The same was true in identifying their modes.   The reason why the medieval church modes, such as Phrygian and Dorian, do not agree with those of the Greeks was because of a mistake by Boethius in the 500s of the Common Era. He thought the Greeks were thinking upwards. (Still more about Boethius later on.) It should be sufficient to say that the Medieval Ionian mode was really the Greek Lydian mode. Carrying through with further parallels would prove little for our purposes here. The Greeks also had a complicated "hypo" and "hyper" system of modes that related to their Dorian, Phrygian and Lydian modes. (As mentioned earlier, this probably accommodated the different voice ranges.) From that, the later Medieval theorists would create what they called plagal modes. Each of the Greek modes also had a sort of theoretical reference tone called the mese, and probably that in turn oriented the compass of the performers' voice, and the scale formation as "positioned" on the Lyre's, or Kithara's particular range.

MORE ON THE TETRACHORDS
Using modern letters for notes, and arbitrarily starting with our fixed A, the Diatonic genera would be A – G - F – E. The Chromatic would be A – G# - F and E. The Enharmonic would be A – F – F – E. The two Fs would be different pitches, but only slightly so.   Another way of getting closer to the Greeks' way of thinking is to begin with an arbitrary pitch, descend a major 2nd, then another major

2nd, then a minor 2nd, and you have the Diatonic shading. Begin again with that same starting pitch, descend a minor 2nd, then an augmented 2nd, then a minor 2nd, and you have the Chromatic. For the Enharmonic descend a near minor 2nd, then a minimal micro distance, then a minor 2nd. The two closely pitched notes would be close enough to create beats. And as I suggested earlier, the difference in the two close pitches in the Enharmonic shading (genera) would be rationalized with complex mathematics. The Greeks undoubtedly liked the Pentatonic effect, as well as the use of absolute micro-seconds. When, and if they stacked several such matching tetrachords, the result could be an incipient Pentatonic scale formation, or at other times a scale that would sound non-diatonic to our Western European ears. In any case, use of any of the shadings could easily have resulted in a music that would sound to us more Oriental than Occidental.   We must occasionally remind ourselves that the Ancient Greeks were more Oriental than we are accustomed to think. For instance, the Greek colonies of Phrygia, Lydia, Ionia and more were on (what is today Turkish) Anatolia, and had been in fact conquered into the ancient Persian Empire well before Democracy was initiated over on mainland Greece. The Greeks could not have been so close to Persian music without at least some absorption, if not some outright adoption of their sounds into Greek culture. Singing in micro 2nds survives today in the Folk singing of Asia Minor and in nearby Eastern European countries. Recent Television documentaries have shown that tribesmen in near Eastern countries still speak of Alexander as part of their folklore.

The Greeks had differing kinds of modulation, such as 1.) changing from one shade of tetrachord to another shade, 2.) to change from a conjunct to a disjunct tetrachord (no pivot tone), 3.) changing the chanting tone, 4.) changing the mood/ethos, and 5.) probably any other method an imaginative musician could devise to enhance the effectiveness of the poetry. During Alexander's life, writer Aristoxenus in trying to make sense of existing Theory, criticized micro 2nd tuning, and recommended tuning by ear.   At the same time there was a conflicting group who believed in the strict mathematical approach that had been advocated much earlier by Pythagoras. It sounds like the universal conflict one will always find between those who practice, and the few who primarily "theorize."

GEOGRAPHIC LABELS

Concerning the labels Dorian, Phrygian, Lydian and Ionian: Apparently names were assigned to modes representing only a few of the many named Greek City States and regions. Perhaps those few employed designated scalar tunings. Consider Dorian mode representing Doria the large far-western Grecian peninsula having Sparta, Mycenae and Argos; and Phrygian, Lydian and Ionian modes representing towns or locales in Anatolia (modern day Turkey). These modes probably also meant not just tuning, but a mood and a manner of singing with certain melodic motives, perhaps denoting music with the particular geographical flavor. It is an open question why the area of Athens did not have a modal designation, such as "Attican." Either none originated there, or perhaps their tuning and repertory was a blend of all. Or, maybe it was that Athenian music was regarded as the centrist point of reference, and beyond labeled categorization.

While the Greeks thought downward in their Theoretical listing of scales and pitches, the music they created could move in any direction. Please remember that when considering the systematization about to be described. Picture tuning the Kithara, and begin on an A that is in the high tenor range. Then using successive juxtaposed or interlocked tetrachords, tune successively downward notes thereby creating a "scale" that reaches down to, or beyond what we would call an octave. (Interlocked means the bottom note of one tetrachord is simultaneously the top note of the next.) When reaching the bottom, an extra lower notes could be added. With interlocking overlaps, we can well imagine the unusual scalar formations that might result. With the Lyre, or wider ranged Kithara so tuned, the performer could perform, while playing in unisons or an octave away.   Whether harmonic accompaniment existed has never been fathomed. More than likely different performers would probably have used their kithara strings in various other accompanimental ways, such as pedal notes or strummed groups of strings. If there was unison melodic playing while singing, he singer's words, motives and rhythms would have to be somewhat more elaborate than the instrumental notes, but the listener, attending to the poetry, would not have noticed or minded.

8

Even today the free approach to rhythm employed by solo singers, while accompanied, remains a challenge to write down in precise rhythmic notation. Then, as now, there was the potentially plain melody, with the elaborate version sung simultaneously by a performer.

An unusual tuning practice will be described that enables us to see how musicians then matched their voice range with their chosen melody and instrument. Picture (or write on a staff) an eight-note scale that fills the range of the Lyre or Kithara. Often those instruments had a one-octave range. (The Lyre was the lower pitched of the two and seemed to suit the more common performers.) Then tune the scale so that the octave lowest note (and here we will use our modern do – re – mi – sol – la thinking as a point of reference.) would be re. In this and later steps always add accidentals when necessary to conform to our modern major scale. To our way of thinking it would result in a Dorian mode. Then, keeping the same octave framing notes, create what we would call a Phrygian mode. Then framing notes fa --- then sol ---, etc. That gives you a general idea how tunings accommodated a particular voice range, mode of music and instrument. This would also be a form of possible "modulation" they supposedly practiced. (Caution: Their use of the words Dorian, Phrygian, etc. completely differ from modern classroom usage.)

The ancient Greek approach to tunings within that octave could be yet more complex by our standards! Supposedly twenty-one pitches were possible within that theoretical octave, and going further, "tonos" or "tonoi" involved transposition of such potentially complicated scales (something like the process described in the above paragraph). However, whatever scale they chose, there was a fixed vocal pitch point, or note, known as the "mese."

THEIR "GRAND STAVE"
The Greeks would naturally be interested in the total availability of note ranges, so they came up with the so-called Greater Perfect System, not for actual music, but for Theoretical reasoning. It would be something like the way we can think of a Grand Stave: a field of operation. Successively downward, they juxtaposed four tetrachords in creating a master two-octave scale from the high tenor-range A down to a low baritone A -- the full singing range of men's voices. Extra notes could be added on the bottom. A so-called Lesser Perfect System with only three conjunct tetrachords consisted of about eleven notes, thus making it possible to extract various other "scales" that began and ended anywhere in that range – and all in the interest of creating unique melodies. When Aristotle referred to tense music, he probably meant that it was in the higher ranged notes of the singer and the instrument. Later Medieval theorists, reading the work of the Greeks, would liken the ancient Greek Greater Perfect System to their sixteen-note Gamut of two octaves. Then still later in history, with the same goal in mind, we would conceive of the Grand Stave as a sufficient pitch range for musical possibilities.

Chapter 3 THE PERIOD OF ROMAN DOMINATION,
UP TO THE EARLY COMMON ERA (C. E.) AND THE DARK AGES.

For a period of perhaps 1000 years, roughly from 500 BC to 500 CE, there seems to be no new writings. If there were, they may have been stored in the ill-fated Alexandrian library. Also, it may well be that the Romans, who seemingly added nothing, and respecting Greek intellectualism, passively allowed such books to be retained and supplemented. The Romans, above all, were mostly concerned with tangible practical matters, and mostly saw music as an adjunct to the games. After Augustus' death in 14 C.E., a slow process of internal Empire erosion began. At first there would be a prolonged period of imperial expanse that would eventually see a new Rome created at Byzantium, created sometime after 310 CE. Still later there would be two Caesars, one for the old Rome and its Western lands, and the other to administer the vast Eastern lands with its heavily Greek culture.

That Eastern political center on the Black Sea, with its highly defensible position, would last for over a thousand years, during and beyond the slow failure of the Western lands.   Meanwhile the West would endure a series of devastating vandal and barbarian invasions beginning in 400s CE, and lasting hundreds of years. With very little surviving culture, those were truly the Dark Ages. It took until the 800s, or so, for the West to begin redefining itself and to reclaim its many cultural achievements. On the other hand, the Eastern Empire, with its slightly modified Greek culture continued practically undisturbed until the mid 1400s. But through all the disruption in the West, Church music was being retained and organized in fortified castles and monasteries. No doubt continuity in the Eastern lands, along with religious fervor, helped motivate Church musicians in the West to continue on. Still, the ways in which Church music in the West differed markedly from that in the East raise interesting points.

The extent to which Byzantine music (circa 350 to 1440 C.E.) resembles that of Ancient Greece is a question that has challenged scholars up to the present. After the 313 Edict of Milan, thus permitting Christianity, the Ancient Greek music seems to have survived in such religious forms as the Troparia, Kanones and Kontakia. One can conclude they are the Eastern Church's parallel to the West's Gregorian Chant. But are they? And there are other lingering questions: How old are they? How much do they reveal about Classical Greek music? How closely are they related to the coming Western Plainchant? Where are matching melodies, Greek and Gregorian? The Byzantine Eastern Church had its own insular path of development, and that path seemingly did not lead to a viable written notation. If Music Theory hinges on written music, then it was the Western Rome-centered Church and the activities of its various satellites that led the way.

FALLEN ROME

After Western Roman military might ceased protecting citizens and their civil and cultural achievements, Western Europe endured perhaps six centuries of roving bands of illiterate marauders/plunderers who were often cultural destroyers. Indeed some were tribes that would plant roots and eventually create new states that formed the new Medieval Western Europe. The last of plunderers were the Vikings who ravaged for over 200 years, up to the very end of the millennium. Regardless of that, nothing and no one was safe. Apparently plunder was not the only reason for the invaders moving westward. More recent Scientific Research has concluded that drought and famine in the Far East were caused by at least one mega-volcanic eruption on the other side of the globe during these years. That in turn caused crops to fail, starvation, thereby forcing the search for better lands. Hence wave after wave of starving Asian ethnic nations migrated into Western Europe. Hence the fortified castle became the symbol of medieval times. It would be up to the new Roman Christian religion to try to civilize some of the tribes. Its institutions and monks went "underground." Thus, during the long disruptive centuries, many Greek, and Latin writings managed to survive in sometimes remote monasteries. The monks and other religious had their scriptoriums whereby untold documents were translated and recopied. In doing so they also preserved literacy.

It probably was after the legalization of Christianity in 313 C.E. that systematic organization of the Western Church music began, and it is too simple to conclude that it just involved basic hymns, because the Mass ritual negates that presumption. Just how much actual music there was before 313, let alone its organization, will remain mysteries. But, let us suppose that the music that needed organization probably emanated from monasteries. Monastic music was probably already of such a refined nature, that it probably led the way for ordinary congregations to emulate.

Saint Augustine, born in North Africa, was at first a Roman Pagan scholar, and later a convert, eventually becoming the Bishop of the Carthage-region. In about 384 C.E. he wrote extensively, touching on poetry and meter. What he says may have concerned an already existing system of rhythmic procedures that had to have been passed along by rote. Is this an early appearance of Rhythmic Modes that are known to exist in 1100s Paris? No one today knows. Articulate written rhythm would remain a large impediment in music literacy for the next thousand years. Certainly the recitation of poetry would have to have involved long and short syllables, and therefore there had to be a generalized speech rhythm. We are left guessing as to what Augustine meant. While notation innovators found it easier to put a small ink spot (neume) on a writing surface and say it is such and such a pitch, it would remain a problem to establish with symbols just how one neume was held longer than another. So any non-notated, systematized method of rhythm hinted at in the writings of Augustine remains intriguing.

PLAINCHANT FORMATION and the EIGHT CHURCH MODES

That music itself had been accepted by the Church is remarkable, given its earlier association with the Roman Pagan way of life and the emphasis on worldly physical sensation. Evidently over time the early Church fathers, concluded that the Pagan way of life had no ownership of music, and that pious words with coordinated melody was a high form of prayer. After Constantine's acceptance of Christianity in the 300s C.E., the Western Empire Roman Church, through its various conventions called Councils, gradually standardized all its liturgical practices, including music. We can assume that in the early Constantine years musical hymn-singing during the Mass varied widely. Was it already Plainchant? Were the singers entirely clerics, nuns and monks? No one knows.

Apparently monophonic singing remained the norm. Such music proved its worth because of its simple dignity. And, since the Mass required the priest to announce verses aloud, and since large congregations, needing to say or sing responses, could more easily hear what he had sung rather than merely spoken, music added another benefit. Hence, if he sang a short proclamation, the congregation would sing a reply. In time travelers returning from Greek and Byzantine churches undoubtedly would have reported how effective Chant-like singing was in the liturgy. But whatever the reasons, developments or origins, music in the form of Plainchant hymns and responses seem to have been firmly in place the Western Church early in the Common Era. And the melodic contours of these melodies were probably plainly syllabic and far simpler than what eventually evolved, especially in the later practice of multiple notes to one syllable.

So, continuing through the Dark Ages, and in spite of occasional disruptions and invasions, Plainchant hymn-like melodies were steadily transformed into the more elaborate forms of Plainchant we find preserved by the Solesmes scholars of the 1800s. (More on them later.) These transformed versions are elaborate melodic lines that were easily beyond the abilities of ordinary congregational Mass-goers of the early Church. Texts for the various religious ceremonies were taken from the Bible and in numerous cases new prayers and responses were created by the early Church fathers. All of these texts, and perhaps a year-long calendar as well, were in place early on, so that the singing and speaking of these texts were calendar-appropriate. In the monasteries daily life meant marking parts of the day with periodic prayers that were sung.

With regards to text, Chant lines seem to fall into three categories: syllabic, neumatic and melismatic. Syllabic lines have mostly one note to a syllable, neumatic has an equalized spread between one note and several per syllable, and melismatic has consistent numbers of notes per syllable. Seen in the monastic setting, one can more easily accept the development of some rather elaborate melodies. But still, there are questions that will remain forever unanswered. For instance, were they from the Eastern Church? Who composed the melodies in the first place? Groups, as such, do not create music.

Most ancient Plainchant melodies were at the time regarded as ineffable, and today we are forced to regard them as phenomena. But, just as in the case of folk melodies, some individual, or individuals had to have been the creators. So, forever cloaked in religious anonymity, the actual melodic creators of the bulk of the earliest Plainchant will remain permanently unknown.

(There are those in the 20th and 21st Centuries, who through listening to compact disk recordings, regard Plainchant as a high form of peaceful musical pleasure. It is easily one of mankind's highest musical achievements.)

MORE ON THE EIGHT CHURCH MODES
If Plainchant was being sung all over Christendom, conflicting practices could no doubt have resulted. So, inevitably Rome would insist on official organization. What is today called Gregorian Chant is so-labeled because its coordination and organization supposedly took place during the pontificate of Gregory I in 590 - 604. In reality, by 590 there had to have been preceding reformers in various religious centers. So, we can easily conclude that Gregory was organizing music that was typical of certain locals, passed along by rote, and that needed Church-wide proliferation and coordination. It is likely that Gregory officially recognized what had already been mostly in place, and initiated moves towards further standardization. Rightly or wrongly, succeeding centuries would credit that pope with Plainchant organization. The work he started continued well after his Pontificate. He also established what was probably the first official school in church singing, then, and still called the Schola Cantorum.

Another quandary in dealing with Chant and its early organization is the precise time that the eight Church Modes came about. We are led to conclude, that without written notation, the modes were organized earlier than Gregory's pontificate in the early 600s. And without melodies written down in any way? It raises questions. The 1800s Solesmes monks in France, in conducting their massive restoration of Gregorian Chant, created chant versions that are in today's Liber Usualis, and are still used today (in the reduced usage typical of the post-Vatican II Church). The highpoint of Chant formation and scale organization supposedly dates from the 800s, about two centuries after Pope Gregory's work. But, how would the Solesmes monks be so sure of their findings? Was there an 800s crude form of notation in the manuscripts they studied? And were the melodies associated with the sacred texts so well known that the 1800s monks knew the exact melodies by just looking at possible staffless scribblings in 800s manuscripts? Another possibility is that the 1800s monks had access to later attempts at notation that were in place in the later medieval period. Their restoration still leaves more questions. How much of the Solesmes' organization was authentically 800s, and how much was innovated in modern times, especially when it comes to rhythm?

Rather than the Chant melodies, let us here consider the eight Church modes in the 800s, though their organized existence evidently came about centuries earlier. The eight modes were really four sets of pairs, the plagal forms being for lower voice ranges. How much of the reasoning was influenced by the ancient Greek writings? We know that early scholars in the Church were interested in what the Greeks had written, or more accurately what Boethius had transmitted in the 500s. Did that concept exist sometime after that? And if so, were there always eight? One thing is sure: The Church musicians of the 600s or later did not completely invent the concept of modes. For now, we must accept the Solesmes' claim that the scales for Chant melodies involved the (Boethius defined) Dorian, Phrygian, Lydian, and Mixolydian. (In our modern thinking Dorian is the white keys of the piano D up to D. Phrygian E up to E, Lydian F up to F, and Mixolydian G up to G.) Each was eventually paired with a lower range version using the same notes. Each lower version would be Dorian Plagal, Phrygian Plagal, Lydian Plagal, and Mixolydian Plagal.

According to the Solesmes monks, the ancient Church did not use those names. It makes sense, seeing that the Church would not want its sacred scales linked with Ancient Greek mythology. Instead, the Church modes were identified in the above order with numbers (Formerly Dorian is the 1st mode, Dorian Plagel is the 2nd mode, Phrygian is the 3rd mode, its plagal the 4th, etc. The Plagel modes are thus 2nd, 4th, 6th and 8th.) It did not matter that Lydian modes with their B flats were producing the sound of (what we would call) a major scale. To the minds at the time, if a melody were oriented to an F, the mode was Lydian. Further, the singers would, without the concept of an accidental, always create B flats, rather than sing the hideously regarded tritone relationship with the F. To sing altered pitches that disagreed with the written was regarded as false music (musica ficta), and was seemingly a standard practice. Improvised pitch alteration was evidently widely practiced on into the 1500s Renaissance.

Somehow, and sometime during the earlier lawless centuries before 850, the Church oversaw organization of the vast body of melodies into the eight described modes. That meant that each of the many Plainchant melodies would fit into one of the eight modes. The final note of each Chant would indicate the mode it was in. (D for the 1st and 2nd modes, E for the 3rd and 4th, etc.) By modern standards (Schenkerian linear analysis), there is no melodic pattern whereby the final note is indicated. Aside from frequently used motives, the melodic movement is rather random. (A cursory examination of some Phrygian melodies revealed C being tonicized, rather than E.)

Chapter 4 THE CAROLINGIAN RENAISSANCE

The Carolingian period during the 800s, the time of Charlemagne, is considered a small and temporary reawakening of literacy and culture. Even ink was being reintroduced. Celtic Cluniac monks had emerged from a small Irish island that had been untouched by the roving illiterate, culture burning tribes. In their isolation the island monks had kept Greek/Roman secular culture safe and suspended. The Viking raiders had been continually destroying most attempts at cultural progress. It would take centuries before stronger centralized monarchies were able put an end to the Viking problem.

During this same period, while Europe was largely backward, cultural literacy flourished in the Eastern Roman Empire, and in Bagdad, where a comparatively advanced culture was centered. This was made possible by the relative peace that prevailed in those regions. The pre- Islamic Middle Eastern culture was thriving in its way in mathematics, architecture and in certain sciences. The later fledgling Islamic movement would continue that advantage, in spite of the wars of conquest against all of the Roman lands. Travelers and later Crusaders returning to Western Europe would report on the Middle East cultures they had witnessed. The Cluniac monks were probably not the only preservers of literacy during that same 800s period. No doubt other remote monasteries in the vast and growing Christendom were preserving and recopying priceless manuscripts, both religious and secular. But apparently it was the Clunaic monks who traveled and reintroduced culture to the mostly illiterate Clerics and aristocracy in Western Europe. They also founded new continental monasteries.

ADVANCES IN NOTATION AND PRACTICAL NOMENCLATURE

Around 850 Auralianus Reomensis wrote of the already existent organization and character of the Church Modes. No doubt he was building on what Pope Gregory had begun. As said earlier, we are deprived of specifics concerning the earlier organizational process, but by the mid 800s C.E. the modal (scalar) system was apparently in place with each melody categorized, and still without a notation system. Let us appreciate that a tiny portion of mankind without written notation, and with inherent music skill and inexplicably accurate musical memory, for centuries, faithfully passed down melodies by ear intact? It would seem so. We can easily see the organizers (described above) relying on Boetheus to gain ideas about modes, but when the early Christians formulated their interpretation of those writings will remain a mystery. It certainly is an instance where misreadings led to starkly new and effective conclusions. Continuing questions remain: Did the modes come about through contact with music in Constantinople and Eastern related congregations, or were the Western Church musicians that independently creative? Through it all one wonders just how the 800s standardization did or did not involve a written notation. Certainly notation was coming, but slowly.

Regino of Prum, writing in in the late 800s, identifies Music as one of the seven liberal arts. Pressure to develop a written notation would come from the training centers and the choir loft. We have to assume that, century after century, singers in the monasteries each taught the next with a religious fervor for accuracy. But still, over immense time, there could easily be accuracy-drift. In chorister training locations that were populated by musically inclined monks, nuns, clergy and acolytes, there would be a need to teach music accurately and efficiently. Therefore a written method had to come about. Manuscripts with crude attempts at notation would indeed appear sometime late in the first C.E. millennium. Some are without a stave, and they show dots for single syllables, and multiple dots for others with only a crude indication of melodic ups and downs, and certainly no rhythmic indicators. These "scratchings" were easily a crude assistance in remembering the sacred chant melodies. Instruction might then have been aided by such written indications. The subsequent challenge was to improve on that crude written method. Still, progress was slow during the 800s and 900s. By the end of that first turbulent C.E. millennium we have a fixed music of Plainchant music and a crude pitch notation on parchment. Each chant melody was regarded as sacred and therefore above any sort of change. For many coming centuries unchanging Chant melodies would be referred to as Canti Firmi.

What about secular, non-Church music? Other kinds undoubtedly existed, but being deemed unworthy, would never be officially Church-acknowledged or verbally described. At that time, what little resources and effort that existed would be spent only on sacred music.

HUCBALD

Around 875, some 20 years after Reomensis, a writer we know as Hucbald, speaking of musical practice that was common in his day, describes his notion of the Greek Greater Perfect System with its tetrachord reasoning. But, evidently he dropped the tetrachordal thinking of the Greeks, listed the established eight scalar modes, and described intervals and a concept of consonance and dissonance. He may well have crystalized musical practices common to his day. However, he had no access to an accepted written notation for music. In describing the singing of monks, he also may have been the first to acknowledge simultaneously different lines in performance. (Polyphony/Counterpoint) He also discusses intervals, consonance and dissonance, and advocates contrary motion in what he calls organum. For centuries monks had been singing the established chant melodies, and it would appear that certain simultaneously counter lines were creeping into the practice. It most certainly involved newly improvised music simultaneous with the changeless Plainsong melodies. Those newly created extra musical lines would in give rise to most if not all of the Theoretical writings that followed.

ENCHIRIADIS AUTHOR

Around 900 an ANONYMOUS writer (anonymity reflecting the Church's discouragement of personal fame), created the Enchiariadis Manuscripts, an invaluable window on the musical practices in the late 800s (or possibly a little before). In it an incipient counterpoint/harmony appears. It consisted of the cantus firmus and a counter-line and was referred to as Organum. An attempted notation in it employs a form of Daseian notation (Greek letters for notes). So far, this is the first written evidence of simultaneous different voices. The musical examples involve a second voice moving a perfect 4th above the original chant melody so as to form mostly parallel motion in the same rhythm as the chant.   There easily could have been more advanced voice movement, but the limited notation prevented it from being recorded. There are other layers in octave doublings. All voices move in parallel, homorhythmic motion.

ODO Around 920

In his <u>Dialogue on Music</u>, Odo of Cluny (or one of his students) was probably the first to label successive scale degrees using the letters A through G. There were probably other teachers of the time who taught music using those same letters, but when they reached the notes an octave above the first seven, they were labeled H – I – J, and so forth. Without knowing it, Odo was in essence ascribing numbers to each scale degree because the letters A through G also imply numbers 1 through 7. So this was a profound step towards a workable written music method, as well as towards ideation of heard sounds.   It opened the door for further developments. Working with a monochord, Odo also re-discovered and reaffirmed what Pythagoras had described in Classical Greek times: the tunings of the whole tone, perfect fourth, perfect fifth and the octave.

STAVE LINES

Odo's innovations also made possible the first steps towards a stave that would come in the late 900s. First there would be one line to indicate an F (a workable point of reference note in the baritone/tenor vocal range). We can easily picture some of the earliest manuscripts with many notes on, above, and under a single line. In subsequent manuscripts there would be two stave lines, then three, etc. Eventually the pentagram (four-line stave) came about. Dots (note heads/neumes) would appear on and between the stave lines, and they would be the first stave-related written note symbols, using the new scalar alphabetical labels. Alas, rhythms would remain neutral to the eye, and it would take a few more centuries before a given note symbol would be understood as twice as long as another note symbol.

Another ANONYMOUS author (perhaps a contemporary of Leif Erickson), writing around the year 1000, and probably building on what Hucbald had written two hundred years earlier, describes the eight church scalar modes. We should remember that in history the music always existed first. Then after observation, descriptive writings followed. Therefore what this writer describes had logically been in practice for some time during the 900s.

ORGANUM

A later manuscript dating from the 1000s reveals a slight improvement over the Enchiriadis practices, in that the second voice that is somewhat freer in its position over and under the chant melody, and in its melodic direction. It may be that the actual musical practices were more advanced than what was indicated in the manuscripts. There would always be notation limitations on what could be written down. Evidence of more advanced musical practice exists in the form of other manuscripts from the 1000s. They seem to match the more advanced practices typical of music in the then existent pre-Notre Dame Parisian church. Still, it is likely that the notated manuscripts probably show only a minimum of the musical effects in use at the time.

GUIDO

Important steps towards pitch specific (diastematic) notation will come in the 1000s. As was said earlier, the Church music needed choristers and music leaders. And for music instruction to be passed along and to be performed more efficiently in the church/cathedral choir lofts, it would need certain concepts. Chief among the needs would be efficient labels for scalar degrees -- labels that would imply progression up or down. Singers would never sing using the labels A through G. Those labels helped with the stave development, but not in the act of singing. Something more practical was needed. The ancient Greeks had used polysyllabic scalar labels that were not a good example for the Church musicians to emulate in training singers. While the Greeks had shorter ones for singing (toh – teh – etc.), they did not imply progression up or down. Innovation was needed.

Guido D'Arezzo rose to the need, and his methods helped bring about a more specific notation. An innovative teacher, he was obviously fully involved in the training of church choristers. Writing about 1020, he established some useful clear points. He needed an obvious scalar unit with which to teach. So, from the Plainchant *Hymn to Saint John*, he extracted six rising notes and their Latin syllables that begin phrases: They were Ut – re – me – fa – sol – la. (The guttural effect of ut would eventually be replaced with "do" by later musicians.) Each phrase of the hymn begins on a successively higher pitch. Notice that this creates a hexachord, and it also forms most of what we would later call a major scale. Guido's two invented concepts, syllables and hexachords, made music much easier to teach.

The scale that was subsequently built upon was 1-do, 2-re, 3-mi, and so forth up to 6 -la. While it seems simple, such a method eluded previous vocal teachers. It was also an important milestone in the advance of written music. To get what we would call a transposition of the same sound, they could start a hexachord on G, C, or F. This therefore is incipient modulation. To our ears each of the three hexachords sounded like the first six notes of the major scale. In the case of one starting on F, they would merely tune the B with the sound of a flat. It was probably at this time that any sounding of the tritone, either melodically or harmonically, was deemed unacceptable. It was to them a "devil" of a sound, and it would be cautiously avoided for centuries to come.

Guido also established the Gamut, an equivalent of our Grand Stave. It started on what we would call G in the Great Octave, and extended up to E^2. The hexachord could begin on G, C or F, thus six overlapping hexachords would fit in the Gamut. Since his six note unit could begin on two other pitches in the "gamut," specific pitches in various octaves would be identified with multiple syllables to identify which octave it was in. For example Great C could only be C fa, an octave above could only be C sol ut, and C2 could only be C sol fa. For Guido any pitches an octave higher than the basic low hexachord would just be parts of another overlapping hexachord, with multiple syllables to acknowledge the different roles it played in each.

There were several points that were vague in the minds of Guido and his contemporaries, but for the time being those things did not matter. One vague point was in recognizing that the use of A through

G on the stave was another way of thinking progressively 1 through 7. Another was that pitches an octave higher could have the same syllables. And always, whether it was eight-note scales, or hexachord scalar units, there would be religious associations involved. Texts and musical effects had to be religiously appropriate. Guido's hexachord would exist aside the tetrachord as the small unit of scalar construction for perhaps the next 600 years. Instrumentalists probably relied more on tetrachordal thinking. (In the later high Renaissance period of the 1500s, there would be writings dealing with eight-note scales existing side-by-side with writings and instruction that dealt in hexachords.)

So again summarizing, and going back to earlier in that first Christian millennium, time unfolded slowly as centuries passed with seemingly little or no writings concerning music. At some point in the early 500s, 250 years after Augustine's writings, there appeared the Boethius writings, mentioned earlier. Not being an innovator, Boethius thought he was merely copying what the ancient Greeks had left. Then after a further three centuries Cluniac monks emerged from their isolation and were of enormous help in the continental Carolingian (Charlemagne) cultural reawakening of the 800s. This would lead to musicians examining Boethius' writings and, in their minds, continuing on what they thought the Ancient Greeks had started.

Chapter 5 THE GOTHIC CATHEDRAL RENAISSANCE:
ADVANCES IN WRITTEN RHYTHM

Another brief renaissance took place in the 1100s. That period was marked by Cathedral building and the first wave of Crusaders returning from their travels. Cultural advances would carry on into the 1200s. At that time Marco Polo would visit the Orient. France seems to have been the center of Occidental culture. OCCITANIA: In the castles of Spain and southern France the culture had become quite cosmopolitan and liberal, giving rise to off-shoot religions, tolerance and liberal philosophies. This was the time of the Troubadours and their monophonic songs with poetry about love. This advanced live-and-let-live culture would be ruthlessly suppressed and destroyed in the early 1200s by the armies of the Pope and the French King. Aside from pretext of stamping out heresy, there were riches and lands to be acquired.

BACK TRACKING:
As was said earlier, sometime during the late 900s, during the Carolingian cultural revival, the practice of indicating specific pitches on stave lines was established. Thus, a major step in music notation was taken. But the notation of rhythms would remain elusive. This period would also be followed by more centuries of raid-disruption by the Vikings. Cultural complacency was shaken by the first Crusade beginning in 1095. Then more cultural advances took place before and after 1100. The intelligentsia of Western Europe was struggling to be once again literate, and to somehow relate to the secular, scientific, and cultural achievements of the Greek/Roman past. And in terms of music notation, there would be much innovation.

Around 1100 major advances were apparently taking place in Paris. Writings by another "Anonymous" around 1150 describe six rhythmic modes of Discant. At last we have something that involves rhythm. But first, what is this Discant? The writer was referring to what we would call a new polyphony. There are enough surviving manuscripts from this period that allow us to hypothesize that, sometime in the 1000s, three contrapuntal textures had come about in Church music, and those textures would continue to develop and be refined for at least two or more centuries. They were 1.) Sustained note Chant line (this texture has many names), 2.) A Chant line with one or two extra voices moving approximately twice as fast as the Chant line, and 3.) Conductus, where all voices move in block chords most of the time. Each of these and their labels will be described later. Each was a new type of multi-voice texture with unique approaches to rhythm. The three textures were made possible by the Rhythmic Modes. These are major steps towards a multi-voice counterpoint, and especially towards rhythmic independence in each of three simultaneous voices.

RHYTHMIC MODES: In this case mode means method or procedure.
Musical dots, or neumes, on previous manuscripts from the 800s and later, whether it be plainchant or polyphony, give no hint as to whether the music was sung in a continuum of steady beats, or merely in ametric equal notes in random groupings. It presented no problem in monophonic singing. But now it mattered more when there were several simultaneous voices singing their own independent lines. Was the polyphony in homorhythmic block chords, with all singing the same rhythm, or was there improvised voice independence? The earliest manuscripts merely raise the question. The issue of rhythm in Plainchant, and in the newly emerging polyphony remains unsettled even today. Were there units of two and/or three beats? Or was the only recurring equal value a single neume (as the 1800s Solesmes monks assert)? We will never know the answer to those questions. But this 1100s Paris document affirms that in its day steady beats were indeed used, and there is the enticing suggestion that contemporaneous manuscripts from other locations other than Paris were similarly performed.

The Rhythmic Modes always involved compound (triple division 6/8 or 9/8) beats, but did allow duple beat meter (2/4). The modes were a way of interpreting long and short notes while reading music the appearance of which looked rhythmically random. The singers would read a line with a mental metric template. Why always triple beat division? Mindful of the Holy Trinity, music of the time was all the more holy if it was in units of three. (For now, ignore the timeless naturalness of simple (duple) beat partials. For the time being the triple interpretations would be the official "Modes" method.) To put the Medieval Rhythmic Modes in a modern perspective, think of each beat as a dotted quarter note. "Long" would refer to a quarter note value, and short to an eighth-note value. Mode 1 was long-short, Mode 2 was short-long, in Mode 3 there are two beats, with long meaning a full first beat, with the second beat being short-long. Mode 4 was the reverse of Mode 3: short-long long. Mode 5 was two beats: long-long. Mode 6 was only one beat: short-short-short.

The Latin texts and placement of single neumes and ligatures (ink-joined neumes) in the music would signal the music readers to think in a metric template into which the notes of a phrase would fit. For instance, imagine a full phrase sung in Mode 2, followed by a phrase sung in Mode 3. Two or three simultaneous voices would sing in perhaps different modes in that phrase. It was by no means a clear method. However, the Rhythmic Modes did serve their purpose in allowing different voices to performing opposing cross rhythms. This was a big step forward in voice independence, and it was another step towards seeking a satisfactory method of written music. What it lacked in specificity, it made up for by providing added incentive to find a better way to notate contrapuntal textures that had become accepted.

There were no master scores. Groups of choristers or soloists performed the lines and harmony of the day by reading their own separate parts. Bar lines did not yet exist. The results allowed a limited rhythmic independence in each of the simultaneous lines. And it clearly required steady equal tempo beats to perform. To modern ears, and in modern transcriptions, there would be the effect of 6/8 or 9/8 meter. Modern transcribers, interested in making master scores from separate parts, and confronted with almost chaotic-looking manuscripts, as was said above, are somewhat guided by the resulting harmony in making decisions. But as was also said earlier, two expert transcribers might still bring about somewhat different versions of the same piece.

Another anonymously written Parisian document from around 1225, some 75 years after the earlier manuscript that describes them, further confirms the existence and practice of the Six Rhythmic Modes. It also describes the three textures mentioned earlier: They were the so-called pure Discant and two kinds of Organum (this word, along with the word Discant, just means counterpoint). These three textures, described below, had been in existence well before 1225. This writer also discusses conducti, motets, and hocket. He is also probably the first to refer to harmony. In doing so he claimed that 5ths and Octaves were the preferred harmonic interval in organum. Like all such documents, it reflects practices that had been in existence for some time. Apparently Church music would always forge ahead of the means to adequately notate the advances.

When discussing contrapuntal textures, be reminded that the Chant melodies were the constant for most, if not all of, liturgical music. Many of these melodies were in fact heard so often that they became second nature to the congregants and performers. Perhaps we in our modern world can only imagine how familiar those ancient melodies were to people in 1200. If they were at church day in and day out, year after year, they heard them again and again. Such familiarity among the singing musicians was an open opportunity for improvisation of extra faster-moving lines by the gifted soloists. Such accretions resulted in counterpoint.

Texture I:
The first kind of Organum is a throwback to the 800s Enchiardis type: Multiple voices all mimicking the rhythm of the all-important appropriate chant melody. Except for minute deviations, all had to have the same rhythm, and remain in ongoing parallel perfect 5ths and octaves. However, such counterpoint would have been easy for singers in different layers to improvise, provided the main chant line was unchanged. The improvised lines, through repetition, would then be memorized. And, just as the Enchiardis document asserts, there was sometimes oblique motion. (One voice moves, the other stays.) Moreover, by the 1200s, and assuming the singers in Paris were becoming more advanced, there was probably some contrary motion, especially at cadences. The important feature was the general effect of homorhythm, all voices in nearly the same rhythm. The later

Conductus form would be the same, except that there are no easily identifiable pre-existent Chant melodies.

Texture II
This had to have involved capable soloists, and in modern times it goes under various labels. Here is an incomplete list: Aquitanian polyphony, St. Martial Style, Pound-note style, Sustained-note style, Melismatic, Florid Organum and Limoges style. This texture is easy to spot in the manuscripts of the time. The cantus firmus moves in obviously longer held notes, while added simultaneous voices are in many dots/neumes. As far as is known, this style was limited to two-voice texture. The elaborate, melismatic added lines were performed fast and had to have involved soloists. Two talented improvisers could well have created three-voice textures, but the surviving manuscripts show only two voices. Likely what was actually performed far exceeded what survives in ink.

Imagine a typical passage in Chant that was itself syllabic in that there were one, two or three notes per text syllable. Now imagine the full choir singing each of those notes deliberately slowly while a gifted soloist improvises a very fast melismatic line of 5 to 7 notes per bottom voice syllable. And they do this pitch-wise above the chant. Additionally, that fast line would be in the compound triple beat described above. The soloist was easily thinking successively in one or more of the six rhythmic modes. As was said earlier, the notation of such a texture (having approximated what the soloist improvised) can be easily spotted in any manuscript from the time. However, this texture could not be used all the time because it extended the time for the performance of the all-important Chant melody, and it would have the priest waiting unduly to go on with the Mass. Then, as now, there had to be practicality in the music from the choir loft. So, when the particular chant being enhanced had melismatic portions with many notes to text syllables, Pound-Note style would then be avoided because it unreasonably extended the time of performance. That is how the so-called Discant Clausula came about. If and when a chant went into melismatic style, the choir would then go into the third Organum texture, about to be described. Surviving Parisian manuscripts from this period, and specifically portions involving the Propers of the Mass, reveal an alternation between these two textures.

It is obvious that Texture II pushed the advance of music because of its use of two obviously and radically different simultaneous speeds. And how old was this Texture II by the 1200s? An earlier manuscript from England from the 1000s in barely decipherable and staffless notation is in two voices with one slower voice expressed in dots, and a markedly faster simultaneous voice with many dots. The earlier date of this particular manuscript suggests this texture was being used well before its Parisian use in the 1200s. While the vague notation in the older manuscripts teases and challenges would-be modern transcribers, the Parisian manuscripts show a clearer picture of specific pitches and relative rhythms.

TEXTURE III ---DISCANT CLAUSULA
This contrapuntal texture emanates from the pre Notre Dame church in Paris in the late 1100s, and is easily a prototype of later music developments towards the motet in the following 1300s and 1400s. The differential in speeds between the lines is not that great when compared to the Pound-Note style. The surviving manuscripts are always in the form of single parts. (There would be no master scores for hundreds of years.) Discant Clausula more obviously used the six Rhythmic Modes. A very early version, probably around 1170, is in two voices. Picture the majority of the choir, with instrumental help, performing a neumatic chant line, while the performers reading another neumatic single line, and interpreting the speed pattern of the notes in the manner of the Rhythmic Modes. The Chant line, going slower than any added lines, was in one of the slower Rhythmic Modes, and might well present a repeating pattern in the manner of an ostinato. (Beat – beat – beat – rest) Modern transcriptions have the Chant line moving in dotted quarter-notes, with the faster voices moving in eighth and quarter notes. Perhaps, with our modern ears, we would sometimes hear 6/8 meter, and at other times 9/8, and perhaps irregular in seeming in one meter or the other. Certainly there was a regular continuum of what we would call dotted quarter beats.

When would they have employed the Discant Clausula method? It would not be used in the Ordinary of the Mass, but rather during one of the Propers. (Proper to the day.) If the Chant line were mostly syllabic, the added lines might well be in Pound-note style. However, if the Chant line presented a melisma (many notes to a syllable), and, as said earlier, the added voices would prolong the music unduly. So, instead, Discant Clausula was used to get through the melisma faster. (Keep in mind, the priest is waiting for the music to end.) In Textures II and III an added voice, newly composed, and more than likely sung by a one or a few singers, would be above the Chant line. The alternation of Pound-Note style with Discant Clausula during the Mass easily provided a satisfying musical effect.

LEONIN and PEROTIN

Two voice texture was common. The first voice added to the Chant melody was called the Duplum. A potential second added voice was the Triplum, and a less frequent third voice the quadruplum. Because the earliest manuscripts show this texture in only two voices, and since an almost off-hand comment in a manuscript of the time says that music director Leonin was succeeded by Perotin, credit (rightly or wrongly) is given to Leonin for two-voice texture. Any three or four voice versions are seen as outgrowths and are credited to Leonin's successor Perotin.

The harmony of simultaneous voices was relatively free, provided that at beat attacks, perfect 5ths, octaves and occasional 3rds up from the cantus usually prevailed. If there were more than one voice above the cantus, they could occasionally bump against one another dissonantly anywhere other than beat attacks. Dissonance was thus somewhat tolerated in the fast voices between beat attacks. Parallel 5ths and other parallel movements were accepted.

TROPING: Inserting texts

What words were used in these added voices? Apparently improvised extra Latin phrases, words and syllables that were closely, and sometimes remotely related to the Cantus Firmus text. The text could be a related prayer. Adding any texts to the already fixed liturgy was one kind of trope. Troping could take place during a normally single voice Chant. Instead of singing one syllable on an eight-note melisma, it was simpler for the singers to assign a separate syllable for each note. Apparently the Medieval mind also accepted syllables and words that would be, to us, inappropriate or incongruous. For instance a Latin text in the Cantus dealing with the Virgin Mary, might well have the duplum or triplum singing about secular situations involving a woman.

MOTET

A Discant Clausula having a Duplum or Triplum that used vernacular language (French) was called a Motet. Eventually that led to stand-alone motets. In time, while the origination of motets was either forgotten or taken for granted, the motet itself would continue evolving in succeeding centuries. The word Motet was eventually taken to mean any sacred and dignified sung prayer.

When listening to modern recordings of Leonin/Perotine music, with its alternation between Pound-Note and Discant Clausula textures, we hear a profound and timeless beauty. Documents from this time also describe other textures, such as the so-called Conductus, mentioned earlier and described as a homorhythmic organum textural type. Conducti are perhaps the first written examples that use no Chant melodies. There is also the so-called Hocket, a texture of hiccup-like note alternation between multiple voices. Evidently Church Music was becoming less monopolistic. Considering typical humanity, we intuitively know that secular music did exist, though no records blatantly say so. Comments in Parisian writings and Manuscripts from this period seem to insinuate its existence.

The music created in the Paris of this time had grown into so-called Square Notation with neume groupings and phrases called ordos that were to be interpreted by singers employing the Six Rhythmic modes. Each ordo usually stayed with one of the modes (repeated long-shorts, or repeated short-longs, etc) The Rhythmic Modal system, then and now, was and is a vague way of indicating rhythm, subject to individual interpretations. However, it would do for the time being. Since French music then thrived on Trinity-like metric effects, it would have been impossible to avoid hemiola rhythmic effects. (Two faster triplets fitting into a slower triplet.) It is a timeless metric relationship that any talented improvising performer would exhibit throughout history, and its ubiquity would be evident up to and including the 1500s and beyond. Though creating modern transcriptions of scores from these Parisian Manuscripts is a daunting task, the wise transcriber will always include hemiolas when possible.

ISORHYTHM: (A repeating metric ostinato)
The bottom voice, the Chant melody, as described earlier, always stayed in the mode with the longer-valued notes (long-long-long, etc.) In the course of time, the bottom voice, in order to fill out the ordo satisfactorily, made use of regular recurring rests, for example: long-long-long-rest. This repetition seemed to act as a metric ostinato. In time this practice gradually turned into what later is called Isorhythm. The Isorhythmic Motet was a staple of the 1200s and 1300s. To make these ostinatos yet more obvious, a drum was used, playing along with the bottom voice singers. Though singers followed conducted beats, the use of a drum ever more so emphasized a beat-rhythmicality that cried out for a written symbol that firmly indicated the beat, as well as other symbols that indicated beat partials.

JOHN GARLAND
Around 1240 An Englishman teaching in Paris informs us that the religious instrumental music of his day was more agile and chromatic than the choral music. He also describes organum (counterpoint) and how the a 3rd and 4th voices worked. He describes harmonic consonance and dissonance, and especially (the new assertion) that 3rds are considered consonant. He described "copula" as being a created voice with a continuum of single phrases separated by rests. Garland speaks of copula as a voice that was coupled with a Chant line. But Garland's contemporaries did not agree on his definition of copula. Another source says that in the 1100s a copula meant a cadence with a coupled voice. Garland, in his own way, explains that what we would call beats, must have consonant harmony in the form of 5ths and 8ves. Other harmonic intervals, such as 3rds and 6ths are to be used on the off-beats. He discusses the Six Rhythmic Modes, and advises that ligatures (ink-connected notes) with more than three neumes should move in fast motion. (In later times we might call these examples of l6th notes) Garland also clarified the length of rests, though his symbols for rests remained unique to him.

FRANCO OF COLOGNE
Around 1250-60, writer Franco echoed Garland in verifying the established rules for creating Motets. He also described the on-going process of composing. Parallel perfect 5ths seem to have been a trait of the music of those times, and Franco endorsed them. He also took a large step in the development of notation by clarifying note symbol durations in relation to one another. This was new. What he said would remain the notational system until sometime in the 1300s when the new method of the Four Prolations came about. Franco's contributions are considered major.

GYMELS AND ENGLISH DISCANT
Perhaps beginning in the 1200s and continuing into the 1300s English composers tended to favor parallel 3rds and 6ths when pairing a new voice with a Cantus line. This practice is called Gymels (twin-voices), and it would continue in European music on into the l800s and beyond. In the late 1200s the English added a third voice to the Gymel motion that was a 6th above the lowest sounding voice. This resulted in what we would later call parallel 6th triads in the interior of phrases. This has come to be called English Discant. Phrases would of course continue beginning and ending with octaves or a perfect 5th and octave. It would seem that the English, in their preference for thirds and triads so early in history, were the predictors of the 1400 – 1500s Renaissance style. With the English in France during the protracted coming war, a co-mingling of styles would inevitably happen. John Dunstable's dissonant-free continuum of triads in the early 1400s was indeed an outgrowth of what had started in England in the 1200s. Dunstable had spent much time in France, along with the English armies, defending what their monarch had rightfully inherited. He was conveniently positioned to influence his French region contemporary composers.

BACK TRACKING:

ANONYMOUS IV
Around 1275 this Englishman, seemingly oblivious to the writings of Franco, wrote of the composers and music of the Notre Dame (Parisian Church) period some 70 years earlier. He, too, endorsed offbeat harmonic intervals that could be dissonant. He was unsure whether 6ths are consonant.

PETRUS DA CRUCE (PETER CROSS?) PETRONIAN NOTATION
Also in the late 1200s, Petrus da Cruce, perhaps an Englishman working in Italy, developed a notational method for writing fast notes on the beat. It was a concept that was well ahead of its time, and seems to predict the method of writing pentuplets, sextuples, septuplets and beyond that would be used in much later Baroque, Classic and Modern scores. His method of notation differed from the contemporaneous French procedures, and was referred to as the Italian way. By the late 1300s there was a mixing of elements of both systems. (More about this later.)

OTHER HAPPENINGS IN THE COMING 1300s
Early in the 1300s Pope Clement V moved the papacy to Avignon, France for, among other reasons, to better deal with the increasingly-powerful French King. The papacy remained there, unopposed until 1378, when for a while there were two or three simultaneous popes in different geographical locations, Rome included. The 1300s would also be a century with three appearances of the plague, and the beginning of the Hundred Year's War. There was naturally a prevailing cynicism everywhere in the face of so much death. Blind faith in religion was being tested. But, despite all the upheaval, progress in all of music continued in Western Europe. Amid the dissolution of morale and loss of life, music was undergoing important changes.

Also early in the century there was a challenge to the succession of French throne. The ongoing Medieval ownership of lands by aristocratic families on both sides of the English Channel had blurred the actual differentiation between England and France. The Capetian family that had occupied the French throne for centuries, was dying out. Then, between 1318 and the mid 1400s, the Plantagenet family, housed in England and France, refused to accept the Valois family inheriting the French throne. This was happening at the time when composers were dropping the need to always include sacred Chant melodies and sacred texts. In a sense, the lid was off the many restrictions concerning acceptable music.

MARCHETTO
In the early 1300s the complete chromatic scale had come about, and a certain Marchetto of Padua wrote of enharmonic spellings. Other steps forward were the development of the portable *Positive* organ in the 1300s, and still later in the 1400s the clavichord. Both instrument keyboards, afforded a more intimate means whereby scales, intervals and chords could easily be pictured and auditioned. Here the chromatic scale could be seen and pondered, and eventually compared with the Ancient Greek writings on chromatic tetrachords. It may well be that growth in a kind of chromatic thinking such as Marchetto's continued underground for the next two centuries, re-emerging in the 1500s in the writings and music of Nicolo Vicentino and Carlo Gesualdo.

CANTELENA STYLE
A voice format emerged that would hold on for centuries: the so-called Cantelina style. (Other names: Ballade, Polyphonic Ballad, Treble-dominated) It was a very early type of monody (melody and accompaniment), and because of its constant use, it seems to unify a long swath of music history. It consisted of three contrapuntal lines. The main line featured a singer in common language (French), with usually two accompanying lute lines. Of course there were other non-Cantelina formats in the 1300s and 1400s, all classifiable under the aegis of counterpoint. But the Cantelina style stands out in its intimacy, appeal, format clarity and metric constancy.

Cantelina Style harmony at first allowed much dissonance, provided there were bass-related perfect 5th and octaves on the beats. As this format/style progressed from its early Parisian 1200s formative days, through its Machaut type in the early 1400s, to its late 1400s Burgundian (Binchois and Busnois) days, it seemed to gradually clarify three-voice triadic harmonic practice. Machaut's music exemplified the French approach in the 1300s, and it was certainly more cerebral in that separate lines mattered far more than any concern for harmonic niceties. Separate voices continued bumping into one another regardless of the dissonance. The Machaut examples are downright harmonically untidy when compared with the mellow examples by his exact Italian contemporary, the blind Landini (or Landino), whose music was laced with triads. The preference for triads will be a major trait of the coming Music Renaissance roughly from 1435 to 1610. Landini combined elements of Petronian notation with that of the French, thus setting the stage for the later rhythmic and musical advances of Dufay in the mid 1400s.

The main voice, the one being sung, moved definitely faster than the two accompanying voices supplied by lute types, almost suggesting chordal accompaniment. Parallel perfect 5ths were acceptable. It was during this period that fourths up from the lowest sounding voice were deemed unacceptable, other than as brief transient instances between beats. While some second-rate composers avoided harmonic fourths altogether, main-line composers accepted harmonic fourths, perfect and augmented, if they were related to an inner voice. In fact all acceptable harmonic intervals seemed to be measured from the lowest sounding voices, and in time that would occasionally lead to occasional seemingly odd relationships between upper voices. It also suggests that the second and third voices were added successively. A prominent feature of Cantilena Style was its double perfection dyad cadences. There would frequently be two-chord endings on phrases in a few variations, such as the so-called Landini under third movement in the highest voice, the Burgundian double leading tones and another practice where a voice leaped an octave from the bass to end as the middle sounding voice.

Another important harmonic development began in England in the 1300s. At the time there seems to have been a close cultural association between Italy and England in spite of their geographical distance. That association is undocumented and not fully understood. The music of both nations exhibits a clearer triadic construction during the 1300s, Landini included. On the continent in the earliest contrapuntal days the third was regarded as dissonant, a premise that seems illogical to us. However, parallel third movement was common in England by the 1300s.

STREAMS OF 6/3 CHORDS: English Discant
The acceptance of what we would call First Inversion chords, sometimes in succession, came about, cautiously at first, and it happened in England. The first step was when a second voice was improvised a harmonic third under and over a Cantus melody. Then in time a third voice was improvised a perfect 4th above whatever the middle sounding voice was, Cantus included. What resulted was a continuum of what we would call First Inversion 6/3 triads, though the thinking of the time certainly did not measure intervals up from the bass to arrive at a 6/3 label. Today, we call such 1300s triadic movement English Discant. Each such phrase would begin and end with a Double Perfection dyad, but the interior of the phrase could have streams of 6/3 chords. The deliberate intent and desire for such parallel triads was clear, and this was far ahead of its time. The very sound itself evidently seduced the French, because by the middle of the 1400s, Dufay had adopted it, albeit with the Cantus in the top voice.

As was commented earlier, it would have been easy for an English composer, on French soil during the Hundred Years War, to influence the native French composers. A particular 1400s English composer was definitely on French soil at the time and evidently influenced French and other nearby continental composers. He was John Dunstable. His music, entirely triadic, avoids any sort of dissonance. The French and Lowlander composers were to eventually blend the Dunstable sound with their penchant for occasional dissonance in arriving at the mature Renaissance sound.

DEVELOPMENTS IN NOTATING RHYTHM

While the way of indicating specific pitches had been established by the start of the 1300s, better, more specific control of rhythm remained a problem. Almost inevitably, two approaches emerged that replaced the Rhythmic Modes. Mensuration is the word that refers to the temporal measuring of note symbols, and progress was slow indeed. Two approaches began in the 1300s, one in Italy and the other in France. Both were a step forward, but that of the French way (The Four Prolations) proved more lasting and would survive in choral counterpoint until about 1600.

During the late 1200s on the Italian Peninsula, a way of indicating beat partials came about, and it was the so-called Petronian (Petrus da Cruce, Peter Cross) notation. Assuming there was still a reverence for the chosen Chant melody and its placement on the bottom, extra created voices above the Cantus could illustrate a wider variety of rhythms. There were remnants of the Rhythmic Modes combined with a simple, yet radically new procedure. Occasional beats showed an upper voice with a variable number of equal quick notes. There could be up to seven quick notes on a given beat. Put another way, an upper voice could occasionally and suddenly sing (what we would call) a gruppetto such as a pentuplet, or a septuplet, all dependent on the number of manuscript dots for that voice on that beat. A glance at his scores shows that these gruppettos did not happen very often, but it was a large step forward when we think of notation in later centuries. This device provided a rhythmic flexibility not heard in the contemporaneous French manuscripts. Already in the 1300s the French and Petronian methods of notation were giving rise to the "three-speed" motet. The cantus would always move the slowest, with the upper two voices in speedier relationships. Maybe in the Petronian method the three-speed differences were more pronounced. Also, it may have been Landini, or someone around his time in the late 1300s who decided that a note with a dot behind it would add extra length to its duration. Precise standardization of that extra length would only come in 1600s.

Concurrently, in France, in the late 1200s the Four Prolations had come into being, and that scheme would be documented by Bishop Philippe De Vitry in the early 1300s, well after it had been in practice. His treatise, entitled Ars Nova, has been accepted to name an entire 1300s continuum of scores, Machaut's included. (More on that later.) Let us think of the Four Prolations as four basic meters, and that each of those Prolations involved extensive metric presumptions (beat formatting – in that a singer read a seemingly random line with a metric template in mind). The Four Prolations would allow music to move beyond limits of the Rhythmic Modes. (More on this later.)

VARIOUS WRITERS:

During the late 1200s and 1300s there were a number of writers who merely reiterated what was already known in their time. Jerome of Moravia, Jacques de Liege, Johannes de Grocheo and Ugolino of Orvieto added little innovation towards the development of harmony and written rhythms. On the other hand, the following contributed significantly in their writings: Walter Oddington, around 1310 divided the 5th to acoustically justify 3rds. He advised composers how to phrase using the old Rhythmic Modes, and he spoke of the two-speed three-voice motet. Marchetto da Padova, around 1315 discussed Petronian rhythm and its notation.

Chapter 6 THE ARS NOVA

Philippe de Vitry, around 1325, in his famous Ars Nova treatise, states that duple meter has now been officially accepted. Though Musica Ficta (improvised chromatics) had been used for centuries, he now speaks of its necessity. Johan des Murs (or Muris?) No. 2, around 1325 was a contemporary of de Vitry's, and agreed with his principles. Murs may be the first writer to use the word Counterpoint. He also says that instrumentalists had their own notation. (We would like to know more about that!) He gives tables of chords, a practice that would continue in future writings by others. He also refers to chords while discussing single voices.

Because De Vitry called his document The Ars Nova (The New Art), the whole era, perhaps 1300 to about 1450, is known as the Ars Nova. It was, according to accounts, a rather turbulent period in France and England, as the French throne claimants and Plantagenets fought it out on French soil for well over 100 years. (The Valois dynasty finally prevailed, and the Plantagenet dynasty in England itself eventually came to an ignominious end in the late 1400s with the defeat of Richard III by the non-royal Tudor clan.) But back in the 1300s in war-ravaged cities, towns and in battle tents, music of a certain kind was being written, the rhythms of which were determined by the newly adopted Four Prolations. Innovators in music notation, whether they be in France or Italy, saw the official acceptance of Duple Meter probably well before De Vitry's treatise. Maybe it first appeared in secular music, but now it was now perfectly acceptable in religious music.   In terms of the continued use of the Four Prolations, we can speak of both the Ars Nova period (1350 – 1450), and the Renaissance (1450 -1600). The very appearance of the neumes did indicate that some were faster than others, but not specific enough when it involved faster moving values.

THE FOUR PROLATIONS

At some time in the 1300s a neume "ink spot" became associated with the heartbeat. The name for it was a breve, and it became associated with one hand-stroke or "tactus" of the choral conductor. We can also relate the breve to a full measure note in modern notation. Any longer held note (two breves worth) would have to be ink-wise twice as long as the heart-beat neume. Notes temporarily shorter than the breve, in time, assumed stems, and these would be regarded as semi-breves. (Two partials in our full measure.) Also, in the late 1300s incipient bar lines would appear in lute and keyboard music. However, these lines were not metric, but rather section indicators. By the mid 1400s hollow note heads (white notes) were used to indicate longer held notes. (They would much later be called half and whole notes.)

Subsequently, as we move into the Renaissance after 1450, notation took on a different appearance. Symbols for double breves, breves and semibres would be ink-outlined, rather than ink filled-in. Faster values such as beat partials and micropartials would remain fully ink-black.   The symbol relationship remained the same as before, except for the new "white-notes." It certainly took less ink, and it allowed for yet more note-length possibilities. It was also a step towards our modern notation with our whole note and half-note ovals.   Somewhat faster notes were then indicated as filled-in stemmed notes. To understand this, picture our half note and quarter note, both with stems, one outlined, and the other filled in. So in retrospect, it was during the 1300s that composers had finally established temporal relationships between note symbols. However, this whole system was still not fully modern because any line of music did not show its intended meter. Instead the performer would interpret the generalized line with a specific metric template in mind.   An illustration would be a skilled reader being able to read the same line successively in each of the Four Prolations, and each time it would be timed differently with regards to the speed of the quicker values in each breve. It was the beat divisions and micro-divisions that were tricky. There would be no master scores, but instead merely separate parts, and without bar lines. In those days the singers must have been very well trained musicians indeed.

THE PROLATION KEY SIGNATURES

So notation for the two periods look different. The Ars Nova had completely black notation, and the Renaissance mixed white and black. The First Prolation's symbol was a C, and its closest modern meter equivalents are 2/1, 2/2 and 2/4. The Second Prolation's signature was a C with a dot in the middle, and its closest modern equivalents are 6/4 and 6/8. The symbol for the Third Prolation was a circle, and modern equivalents would be 3/2 and 3/4. The fourth Prolation's symbol was a Circle with a dot in the middle, and it would correspond to our modern 9/4 or 9/8.

Chapter 7 THE PRIME RENAISSANCE AND THE EMERGENCE OF THE TRIAD

Scholars now point to 1450 as the approximate beginning of Music's Renaissance. (A Renaissance of the visual Arts and Humanistic thinking had begun somewhat earlier.) Dufay is now seen as the first in the new practices, and certain new traits in his music had existed for decades before writers such as Tinctoris, would document them in the 1470s. Maybe it was the English who determined that a constant triadic flow was the proper way to create music. As mentioned earlier, John Dunstable's works in the early 1400s reveal an undisturbed continuum of triads. Most of the triads would be formed using what we would call the white notes of the keyboard. It is probably no coincidence that this refinement in harmony came about with the proliferation of the clavichord. Without having to rely on the loud organ sounds of the day, composers could sit at the quiet sounding clavichord and picture and audition triadic movement.

Dunstable was present in France with the English forces during the Hundred Years War, and his music undoubtedly influenced the French composers of the time. His important contemporary Dufay in his music would then complement the flow of triads with intermingled, temporary dissonance. (And he, and his contemporaries, did not yet think of a triad as a unit.) This process could then easily describe the entire Renaissance Musical model. It would be some later composers who would incorporate imitative lines. While the chosen triads were mainly comprised of what we would today describe as the white keys on the keyboard, there would be no method of determining what order the triads would succeed one another. That achievement that would have to wait for later Baroque composers after 1600. Renaissance composers thus utilized chordal successions rather than progressions.

The main medium for Renaissance composers, and for most the only one, was the choral group, and the need for religious choral music would lead the way for new developments. (Developments that may seem to us quite ordinary.) Dufay and others were still using mandated sacred Chant melodies, around which they would weave other lines in acceptable intervals above the bass line. Dufay started working with what we regard as the standard ("Familiar") SATB approach, with boys singing the topmost parts. The top voice was referred to as the Superious. The Alto (meaning the high counter-tenor). The label Tenor meant the "kept" melody or Cantus Firmus. They then added a newly composed lowest voice that was, to them, the low counter-tenor. The earlier practice of keeping the Cantus as the lowest voice had indeed inhibited the control of harmony. The late 1400s composers found it much easier to weave voices around a cantus that was second from the bottom. Consequently they could more easily control intended triadic change. (Still without a clear concept of the triad in their minds.) Also, there is a strong argument that each of the voices was added successively.

Contemporaneous with Dufay were so-called Burgundian composers who continued the Cantelina-style, monodic works in three voices. But for Dufay and his contemporaries, who were advancing the new way of composing during the first third of the Renaissance, the use of four voices remained obligatory. It was also during the 1400s that Dufay and the others began avoiding parallel perfect 5[ths] between any two voices. Parallel perfect octaves were easy to explain and avoid because of the obvious loss of voice independence at that point. But avoiding parallel 5ths is not so easily explained. Apparently such 5ths movement had become associated with crude music, and was to be avoided because of mere association. Later there would be entertainment choral works in the 1500s that were intended to convey a rustic crudity with their use. For the next 500 years this rule of avoiding parallel 5[ths] would hold fast among teachers and pupils. Dufay and "company" were also careful to treat any 4[ths] above the bass as dissonant. (That, too, would hold for centuries to come.) One could use dissonance in what we would call passing tones and neighbor tones, provided they moved through the dissonance quickly in weak metric positions, and in stepwise motion. And as in earlier centuries, the Renaissance composers continued a practice of putting some parts in different key signatures. These were undoubtedly to avoid the tritone-producing F – B interval.

Two lesser-ranking writer/composers, Prosdocimus de Beldemandis and Bartolomeo Ramos de Pareia, already in the 1400s were thinking and writing about the scale, legitimizing harmonic 3rds and 6ths, and Musica Ficta (mentioned earlier). As usual, such writings really reflected what had become standard practices, and were probably intended for composers-in-training. We know that Musica Ficta had existed as early as perhaps the 900s, but here the practice was being made official. These writers also placed restrictions on the use of harmonic 4ths, and the avoidance of parallel perfect intervals. That more important writer/composer mentioned earlier, Johannes Tinctoris, in the years before 1484 created three books on counterpoint and an encyclopedia that described all the music practices of his day. Whatever rules Palestrina would use a hundred years later are, with the exception of a few details, given by Tinctoris. It is ironic that Tinctoris does not name or speak of the constant use of triads, even though that is obviously the case. He does allow parallel perfect fifths and octaves provided they are necessary, or if they sound good. He also said that cadences (hollow dyads or triads) within a piece should not cadence twice on the same degree.

The music of the entire Renaissance relied on almost random streams of "white-key" triads. So, other than for cadence formulas, as said earlier, there was simply no sense of harmonic progression. Specific diatonic triads succeeded one another in a chance manner. All attention was focused on voice leading and linear contours. Each particular triad is a mere happenstance of the voices moving through it. Let us jump ahead temporarily. Consider Palestrina in the last third of the Renaissance. He continued and refined the style of Josquin Desprez some 50-70 years earlier. Palestrina and his predecessors utilize balanced lines that seem to move like graceful Gregorian chant lines, and each piece would have a number of imitative points where entering voices would mimic one another. Aside from those features, in Palestrina's music there would be an intangible beauty that overcomes the listener. Future writers would fruitlessly try to identify the particular elements bringing this about. His music presents a deliberately "held-back" quality that adds to its beauty, while avoiding theatrical dynamism. To many succeeding musicians and listeners, Palestrina's music was, and remains a paragon of quiet beauty, yet quite distinct from triadic composition of other and later historically important composers after 1600. The "held-back" aura of his music is not merely the result of random triadic successions, but may well lay in his frequent, though not exclusive use of Roots that drop a Perfect 4th. Contrast that with the coming Baroque, Classic and Romantic periods where composers would indulge in ubiquitous Roots dropping by Perfect 5ths. That music would certainly be more dramatic, but alas less prayer-like.

Extending from the end of the 1400s into the beginning 1500s, probably the most important composer was the above-mentioned Josquin des Pres. He seems to have shown future Renaissance composers how to compose. He, and certain of his contemporaneous composers, instituted linear imitation in their choral works. In addition to a number of important composers in this period there were also a number of noteworthy writers. Printing had begun in the middle of the 1400s, and writers' thoughts were increasingly being printed, distributed, inspected and discussed. Often these descriptive writings, reflecting what had been written, merely confirm what can plainly be seen in the scores of the time. Franchino Gafori in the late 1490s, in describing the music of the previous forty years, spoke of the difficulty in logically explaining what sometimes sounded good to the ear. He proposed Equal Temperament tuning, and he described (improvised?) funeral singing that moved in parallel seconds and fourths. However, we have no surviving scores to demonstrate this. He also spoke of another kind of singing that moved in what we know to be parallel triads, though he does not think of, nor isolate the triad as such. This confirms the suspicion that surviving manuscripts show only a partial picture.

PIETRO ARON
While a number of other writers of the time were merely repackaging ideas that were common practice, the writer Pietro Aron, writing around 1520, made some ususual observations: He claimed that composers were no longer creating one voice at a time that agreed with the Cantus, but rather were advancing in their scores, moving four voices at once. It was a vertical procedure that moved forward one beat at a time. Apparently Aron was also the first writer to use the word cadence. He was probably the third writer who advocated thinking in octave scales, rather than in hexachords.

Still, he did not mind allowing the choir directors to continue their particular teaching with their hexachordal, complicated syllable system. Aron also recommended that accidentals not be just improvised, but rather specifically indicated in the score parts. (There still would be no master scores.) He wanted uniform key signatures in all the parts. And importantly, he wanted all musicians to use practical terminology when referring to certain musical devices. (Were the existent terms merely impractical, or did they just vary from town to town?) However, he did assert some things that would ultimately lead nowhere, such as harmony being in either Authentic or Plagal mode. That kind of thinking would end when composers elected to stay within the four SATB voice ranges.

In the 1520s Swiss Hinrich Loris (Glareanus) published writings that reflected how composers probably thought in the previous fifty years. And he probably added a few conclusions of his own. Loris thought in octave scales in a roundabout way. And to the traditional four pairs of Church Modes (review the Eight Church Modes above) he added two extra: Aeolian and the Ionian. Here was the first official acknowledgement of what would ultimately turn into the major and minor scales. Moreover, and alluded to above, any further attempts to explain harmony in terms of particular modes and plagal scale forms would founder. And finally, about one Hundred years after the obvious constant use of triads (mid-1400s), writers were finally beginning to conceive of, and isolate the triad.

Zarlino

Some sixty years after Glareanus, Writer/Composer Gioseffo Zarlino was summing up the music that had been written since 1500 when he wrote about the three-note unit we call the triad. He also reordered Glareanus' six pairs of modes, so that Ionian, rather than Dorian, was first. We can now conveniently picture on our modern keyboard all of the authentic modal forms beginning with Ionian on C, and progressing to Aeolian on A. Here is Zarlino, perhaps in the 1570s, setting the stage for the coming primacy of the C major scale.

In his three tracts published over a thirty year period (1558 – 89) Zarlino proclaimed several other things of note: Music was a unique art, part mathematical and part intuitive, but music should not be subordinated to arithmetic. He was interested in using the monochord to not only rehash earlier findings on intervals, but to explore what we would later call triads. Going further, he classified and systematized all intervals. He related all intervals to the ascending overtone series. While he knew that a 3rd could invert to a 6th, he did not then infer that a root could be the top note of the 6th. A 6th produced, to him, a different harmony. A chord was not a chord, but rather a euphonious combination of intervals. He liked Root Position triads without knowing why. He also knew that First Inversions chords were not totally satisfactory, but could not explain why. For him, the lowest sounding voice was the foundation/fundamental of the simultaneity. But in his limited way, he was thinking in terms of harmony. He probably reflected the way that Palestrina and others intuitively created.

THE PROPER WAYS OF WRITING MUSIC ---

Zarlino published a set of rules and practices for teaching Counterpoint in two and three voices. Allowing for slight individual differences, they were the procedures generally followed by all the major composers throughout the 1500s, Josquin included. Here is a summary of some of the rules, given mostly by Zarlino:

The tactus/heart beat/conductor stroke is still the breve (our whole note). Stepwise motion most of the time in all voices. Though lines in Gregorian Chant could occasionally sound Pentatonic, these lines should not. Immediately fill in leaps. Avoid repeating cells. Avoid tritone contours. Measure all harmonic intervals from the lowest sounding voice. (It is ironic that it took till the end of the 1500s for someone to devise number measurement above the lowest sounding voice in order to control harmony.) There can be 3rds , 5ths and octaves above the bass. 4ths up from the bass should be used as dissonance (passing tones or suspensions). Phrase beginning and ending intervals should be perfect prime, perfect 5ths and octaves. Rarely have simultaneous leaps in the same direction.

Voices should huddle in a space no larger than a 10th. Voices can occasionally cross. The bottom voice should begin and end on the primary modal note. There can be parallel 3rds and 6ths. Avoid parallel perfect intervals. Do not try to create chordal progressions. Notes that are faster than the tactus, usually are what we would call nonharmonic tones, should be approached and left by step. No leaps to or from dissonance. The fastest notes, four times as fast as the tactus, should never be upper neighbors. While notes with a single dot did exist, no other length of note was possible because ties did not yet exist. At the beginning of textual phrases, successive voices enter one at a time and should imitate the rhythm and contour of the first entrance.

Zarlino's set of directions, somewhat oblivious to Palestrina's music, are perhaps 85% accurate. His rules only achieve the same level of accuracy as any other writings, then and now, on the subject. In the coming centuries musical scholars would labor over various methods to learn how Palestrina created his music. Since this is not a book on Renaissance Counterpoint, the reader is advised to study that subject, thereby comparing the Zarlino rules, and 20th Century enlightened set of rules.

Zarlino covered many topics. He classified and systematized all intervals. Dissonant intervals enhanced the consonant ones. He acknowledged compound intervals. (A twelfth is equivalent to a fifth.) Contrary to 20th century thinking, for Zarlino, if an interval was smaller than an octave, it was "simple." A sixth was "compound" because it is made up of two simple intervals. (20th Century Theory defines a compound interval as one larger than an octave.) And reiterating the centuries-old belief, a fourth is consonant, but cannot be used up from the bass in harmonic simultaneities (chords). Cadences involving what we would call major thirds or chords are bright, while those using either a minor third, or what we would call a minor triad are mournful.

AHEAD OF THE MAINSTREAM

In 1529 Writer Ludovico Fogleani, rejected academic tunings and (perhaps) began an era of tuning in temperaments. Pure tunings would simply not survive when chromatics were increasingly be utilized. Writing around 1555, Writer/Composer Nicolo Vicentino thought highly of what the ancient Greeks said about chromatic tunings. While he would create status quo music, Vicentino's Theoretical writings sometimes push for a highly advanced approach. He described the possibility of highly chromatic music, and he spelled all the possible scales using accidentals. He also described cadences on Db, D#, F#, Ab, and B. While the first four of his five books of madrigals are diatonically ordinary, the fifth book is somewhat chromatic for the time. In one spot a voice leaps an augmented third. (One of his pupils, Gesualdo, will carry chromaticism to an even greater extreme.) Vicentino was probably the first to describe imitative counterpoint, though by his day that practice was already fifty years old. He also may have been the first Writer to describe the mechanics of what we call a suspension, though that practice, too, had been around for perhaps 70 years.

In studying the Tetrachords of the Ancient Greeks, and in emulating their chromatic shadings (genera), Vicentino went on to describe his notion of microtones and his way to notate them. He had a microtonally tuned harpsichord. Predictably, contemporaneous Writers disagreed with him on many issues, and they especially claimed he did not fully understand the Ancient Tetrachords.

BACK TO THE MAINSTREAM

Composer/Writer Thomas Morley in 1597 in a section of his book *A Plain and Easy Introduction* demonstrates the combining of imitative lines in madrigals and the like. But aside from that, the writings of Zarlino put a seeming end to Writer-explanations that dealt largely with Renaissance choral music. It is a seeming end because later Writers in coming centuries, ignoring the music of their day, were concerned with just how Palestrina wrote his music. The most obvious of these would be Johannes Fux in the 1720s. But, just after 1600 there were writings that pointed in a new musical direction: instrumental music. Before the late 1500s there had been attempts at notation for instruments such as the lute and the keyboard, but those attempts involved letters, hand-fret positions, and various other complicated systems. By the end of the 1500s composers were writing for the keyboard using notes on a stave.

SUMMARY

So, just what was the state of music in 1599, the near end of the so-called Musical Renaissance? The music of the most renowned names of the time was overwhelmingly in the choral medium. Since about 1550 mainstream composers had favored Counterpoint in five voices, sometimes venturing into six or more. The music was overwhelmingly triadic, and it involved mainly what we would call our "white keys" of the keyboard, with occasionally single "black keys." There was little or no attempt at a system of chordal progressions that would or should recur. Triads merely succeeded one another in random fashion. In Renaissance music, movement forward is achieved through attention to lines and text, rather than by the harmony. In playing through the chordal successions of any Palestrina piece, one is easily struck by a unique beauty that might be poignant and skillful, but not dramatic. Drama would have been vulgar and irreverent. The coming era would turn that reasoning, and its mechanical methods upside down.

Chapter 8 THE BAROQUE PERIOD

Master scores will appear in the l600s, and in them would be the first metric bar lines. Also, sometime in the l600s, and the new emphasis on precise metricism, the use of measurement ties came into being. There would naturally be a need to sustain instrumental notes to any length, rather than just equal, or one half of the value of the starting note. The first signs of Baroque tendencies in music overlapped the period of the nearly spent Renaissance. For instance, the Venetian instrumental music of German Heinrich Schutz, as well as the notation for lute music, and the keyboard music such as in the Fitzwilliam Virginal Book, seem more Baroque than Renaissance. Also late in the 1500s there were attempts to feature vocal soloists in pre-arranged songs that together told a story. In Florence a group of musical aristocrats helped to bring about singer accompaniments involving bass lines with numerical chordal abbreviations, later known as Figured Bass. With the late 1600s development of "appropriate and dynamic chordal progressions" there would be what one scholar refers to as outer-voice (melody and bass line) polarity. The situation was ripe for the further development instrumental music and opera.

FIGURED BASS
Beginning just before 1600, a new kind of abbreviated harmonic notation, its development and improvements would remain throughout the Baroque period, and would survive in private and classroom instruction right up to the present. While at first it assisted keyboardists in performance, this short-hand would also result in the second of three significant numerical systems used to teach the writing of music. (Scale degree numbers from Odo of Cluny's and Guido D'Arezzo's time being the first.)

Composers and keyboardists in the early 1600s were increasingly accompanying their melodies with block chords above a bass line. Those chords could be indicated with stacked numbers indicating what intervals to play above the bass. Now here was something concrete and codified to pass along to aspiring musicians. It would also be the subject of continuing treatises and "how-to" books, starting with that of Hieronymus Praetorius around l617. The triad as an entity would slowly emerge. It is strange for us to think of keyboardists at that time, following a figured bass, and playing what we now know to be Root Position and inverted triads, without knowing much about the actual chords they were playing. But that was indeed the case. Potential writers, though constantly looking at triads on the keyboard, and who were in an ideal situation for discovering inverted triads, were seemingly oblivious. It would be a hundred years later when Johann David Heinichen would write of triads, but only in a vague way. In the mean time all keyboardists always thought of the bass note as the Fundamental of the chord. Being confronted with many – many chords, potential students certainly had a need for some sort of simplifying concept or organization. And indeed some keyboardists were inventing their own systems, with multifarious rules for chordal use.   Their systems were invariably in need of a central unifying principle, and that would come some hundred years later.

TWO NUMERICAL SYSTEMS
Whereas the first numerical system was the numbering of the seven scale degrees (A – B – C – etc, and Do-re-me-etc. became synonymous with 1-2-3-etc.), this new second system was an abbreviation for indicating chords. As said above, the numbers implied harmonic notes in their distance up from the bass. The keyboardist was furnished with a bass line, and usually above each separate note was one or more stacked numbers. If there were no numbers, a keyboard 3 and a 5 (or those intervals plus one or two octaves) would be played above the bass. (Unlike Mathematics, the bottom note was considered "1") We would call a 3 and a 5 above the bass a Root Position chord, but in the late 1590s and on into the l700s, no one thought in that way. Rather these were merely familiar sounding notes above a bass producing a triadic sound. Usually there was no indicated number for the bass note because it was the point of reference. The method was made easier because most of the time there were only (what we would call) Root Position and First Inversion chords. If there was a 6 above the bass note, it meant that there would be a keyboard 3 and a 6, or their octave equivalents, above the bass. They did not think in terms of inverted chords. Even today a keyboardist can successfully and

accurately read figured bass and never think in terms of Root Position or chordal inversions. Far less often there would be a 4 and a 6, what we would call a Second Inversion chord. An example of these two, potentially conflicting numerical systems in a hypothetical chord would be a 6th scale degree which is simultaneously a 3 above the bass. So, an irony: What started an abbreviation also became a method of thinking and teaching harmony to the next generations.

INSTRUMENTAL MUSIC

If Writers were always describing music that existed well before their time, then what Thomas Morley's contemporary, Joachim Burmeister published in 1606 is out-of-the-ordinary. In his treatise Burmeister devoted a section to the methods of moving notes on a stave for maximum musical effect. This was new. He also put labels on types of lines and contrapuntal devices.

What he says was probably aimed at non-vocal music. Significantly, he talks of the differences between the major and minor modes, as if they had become standard, though that was not quite the case. And, important for the coming era, he listed some twenty affections (note movements that bring about moods or emotions) to be used for dramatic effect in music. Operas were now in the picture. Aristocratic audiences were increasingly intrigued with the depiction of dramatic stories with solo singers in dramatic situations, along with accompanying instruments. So, maybe dramatic is the byword for the coming era: the juxtaposition of opposing qualities.

A coming emphasis on instrumental music would not entirely displace singers and texts. Choral and vocal performance would indeed remain prominent. But the doors were opening for a purely instrumental music that was reasoned in its own way. Already in the late 1500s, instrumentalists were demonstrating the pleasing effect of playing many-many notes per beat, and such "note-y" music was firmly established before that century's end. This newly independent instrumental music of the 1600s would later often borrow forms, techniques and mannerisms from the concurrent vocal/choral world. Eventually in that century any one or thing that could perform music, human voice included, was judged by its ability to suddenly stun the listener with brief cascades of notes. These developments would eventually redefine music, and that would come about in spite of the crippling religious warfare in central Europe that impeded cultural growth during the first half of the 1600s.

What was needed in the new era was a tonic chord, and patterned satellite chords to enhance it. The great choral composers of the 1500s had flirted with that notion, and the isolated rare examples of it in their music are not overly obvious. However, maybe one or more English Madrigalists in the early 1600s were ahead of their time. For instance, a complete survey of John Wilbye's music reveals an incipient major tonality with incipient modulations to other secondary tonic levels. However, his music does not indicate a hierarchy of triads.

On the Continent, Johann Lippius, writing around 1612, was well ahead of other Theorists. With his own system of symbols, he seems to have been the first to describe inverted intervals and the triad, which he called a trius. Though the writings of Lippius did not take hold, it would be about 110 years later when around 1725 Rameau, working independently, convinced all that the lowest sounding note (bass) was not necessarily the most important note in the chord. (They needed to think in terms of a Root.) While there may have been others before Rameau who thought that way, he was the first to publicize his assertions, but in the next century. So, we have three important developments, all taking place in the early 1600s: Burmeister's advice on how to handle non-vocal music, late English Madrigalists flirting with major/minor music, and Lippius (almost privately) identifying inverted chords. It was also at this time that bar lines and ligatured beams of quick notes came about. Further study is needed to determine just when and how these developments came about. Certainly instrumental music made it necessary.

FURTHER ORIENTATION

If the 1600s was the Age of Reason, and the 1700s the Age of Enlightenment, then it all seemed to be centered in Paris. At the time, the French nation was the strongest and most prosperous. So, it was fortuitous that intellectual pursuits and learning were aggressively pursued there. That city would thus be the center of the musical reasoning involving composition. There were also simultaneous scholar/writers in Germany staying competitively abreast of what was published in French, and contributing their own treatises. By Rameau's time, beginning in the 1720s, a steady stream of published writings were common, most of it explaining a logic behind the writing of music, and most of it rehashing what had already been established. But this was still the 1600s.

A MATHMATICAL CONNECTION: NOTES
One development in the 1600s Age of Reason was the proliferation of metric divisions. Metric bar lines would come into being, and it would help in the writing and reading of instrumental music. What was more reasonable than marking off regularly recurring groups of beats, especially in view of the many quick notes being used? All through the Baroque period, extending into the 1700s, composers seemed to be fascinated that quarter-note beats could potentially be filled with exactly four 16th notes, or eight 32nd notes, or sixteen 64th notes. (Excessive use of ink, paper and printing man-hours probably held back the use of the fastest notes.) 1600s music frequently involved dotted rhythms and their sub-divisional complexities, jumping from one speed to another, as well as occasional simultaneous combinations of differing fast-note speeds. The "reasoning" of inner subdivisions stimulated and challenged both the composers, and the performers. It seemed that time itself would nicely fit into neat compartments of potential divisions of different speeds. This also meant the clarification and standardization of rest symbols. It became necessary to have an equivalent rest symbol for every durational note. And, while there is no proof of it, performance practice at the time probably involved scrupulously steady beats in order to fully realize that compartmentalized beat organization. Another development was the exploitation of the relativity of note values. While a piece could have the seemingly natural quarter note at the speed of a heartbeat, another piece might have a 16th note, or any other value, at the speed of a heartbeat.

In 1618 Rene Descartes, the eminent Mathematician, when he was not concerned with the ontological argument, would publish a study in overtones and sympathetic vibration. In observing overtones he naturally came upon the triad. He concluded that the perfect 4th is derived from, and is the shadow of the perfect 5th, but it was not equivalent. In a vague way, and using his own words and descriptions, he was dealing with inverted intervals. He said that the minor 3rd is derived from the major 6th. He was also close to discovering the inverted triad without knowing it. The new instrumental music confronting auditors and audiences had no lyrics to guide their apprehension. Thus another Frenchman, Marin Mersenne, who, writing in 1636, and confronted with much emerging instrumental music, advocated listening to the notes themselves to determine the direction a piece of music would take. Certainly the growing audiences for such music would be trying to listen similarly. Mersenne was also involved in numbering the partials in the overtone series, and plotting sympathetic vibrations.

Old habits would die hard. For instance, cadencing on a hollow-sounding "double perfection," (a perfect 5th and octave above the bass), so acceptable in the 1500s, would occasionally appear in 1600s scores that otherwise present constant triads. What would also appear, and remain for the coming centuries of triadic music, would be another, but "harmless" dyad: one that was comprised of only 3rds or 6ths. Also, in 1657 Theorist Christoph Bernhard described a newer, freer counterpoint. To him, the old rules for creating choral music seemed no longer appropriate. In 1687 Andreas Meister endorsed equal temperament, and describes inverted triads without fully understanding the implications. He did not think in terms of a Root potentially above the bass. Alexandre Frere in 1706, and Alexander Malcolm in 1721 wrote of key signatures. Throughout the late 1600s and early 1700s much important music was being written, and in it were devices that needed rational descriptions, thus feeding the need for "How To" books. By the end of the 1600s a figure would appear who would be the supreme master of all the new Baroque traits, Sebastian Bach.

In 1694, momentous comments were made in the writings of Charles Masson, and a little later in that of Sebastian de Brossard in 1703. What they say easily reflects what had been common thinking for some time. In their own way they describe what we know to be a tonic triad that was built on scale degrees 1, 3 and 5: the tonic, mediant; and dominant. Rameau, twenty-five years later, would consult their writings as he formulated his own ideas. It would take much longer for the full standardization of nomenclature of a triad on every scale degree: supertonic, mediant, subdominant, etc.

THE EMERGENCE OF THE PRINCIPLE OF TONALITY
(Chordal heirarchy that make a key sound convincing)

Perhaps it was in the mid l600s that a marvelous development took place, and perhaps no one person could take credit. But by the late l600s, the results are fully evident in the early scores of teenaged Sebastian Bach. What crystalized was a method of harmonizing lines with triads that made the tonic chord stand out as supreme. Many writers of the 20th century have called this TONALITY. If this system were the result of composers hearing overtones, it certainly was not the result of scientific thinking, but rather it was empirical and intuitive with only the merest scientific connection. Later on we will see how Rameau would be able to prove at least a few facets scientifically. The hierarchy of triads in a key, and how they would be used by the major composers, would seem to have very little objective basis, other than their own fixed logic. Maybe it was all based on an acquired conditioning, and maybe not. In any case, Triadic Tonality can be heard in the works of the major composers from Sebastian Bach through Wagner, as well as their contemporaries and beyond. Triadic Tonality thus stands out as one of the major developments in the history of music. It is interesting to note what Rameau was able to prove with overtones. One of his unique claims was that composers first hear the triad, and from that, melody is derived. Other thinkers would oppose him on that point. The standard conclusion was then, and probably is even now, that harmony arises from melody, and not the reverse. Since Rameau was a successful composer, as opposed to merely a thinker, he was probably empirically questioning his own compositional process.

Naturally, and in accordance with what was said above, by 1700 the concepts of major and minor scales had been established. Early in that century Sebastien de Brossard, in his dictionary of sorts, described twelve major and minor scales. Importantly, he claimed that triadic Harmony is the basis of a scale. That is, one can play a triad and then find the scale. (Rameau would later dispute this.) Composers and teachers would not yet see all triads within a key as a field of operation. Teachers would later assign Roman numerals to each possible triad (I, ii, iii, etc.), but in the 1700s composers and teachers did not yet think that way. What we call V – I resolutions and progressions had become abundant, but that practice is insufficient as the major trait of Tonality in the coming two hundred years. In reality Triadic Tonality also involved IV or ii (Predominant function) resolving Dominant function (V, or diminished vii), then to the Tonic. The remaining triads, what we would call iii and vi, would be used as either phrase inserts or substitutes for I, IV or V. So, as harmonic phrases moved along, music would either be progressing towards the tonic, or regressing from it. A demonstrative exemplar would be a perfect progression of iii - vi – ii – V – I, with the Roots resolving downward by perfect 5ths. However, the major composers at that time, operated entirely by ear, and did not think in terms of Roots or Root movement. They were composing intuitively.

A hypothetical example of an extreme retrogression, used here for only demonstration purposes, would be I - V – ii – vi – iii, with Roots resolving upward by perfect 5ths, or falling by perfect 4ths. Music by the great composers most frequently "progresses," with occasional "regressions." But mixed in with these moves are insert and substitute function triads, and "stalling" gestures on a single chord, or a few chords, that make the ideal progression less obvious to the eye. It would, however, make sense to the ear. Another reason is that the important indicative chords are frequently not adjacent. Significant music, in addition to occasionally lingering on functional chords, can in one way or another postpone of arrival at the final Tonic triad in certain phrases, and certainly the piece as a whole.

Figured Bass keyboard books continued to be published, and, until Rameau's writings, were the only attempts at making sense of chordal movement. One such book by Johann Mattheson in in 1731 included information on the "Affections," describing practices that had been in effect for some time. (What they meant by Affections was really what we would call emotional effects -- not a topic for this book.) Mattheson's book, and others like it, were aimed at the keyboard musicians of the time who were non-composing harmonic specialists. But by the time of his book, a few other more momentous publications appeared dealing more closely with the actual composition.

In 1725 a highly seminal teaching method was published by the Viennese composer Johann Fux. It was backward-looking. Evidently he was repelled by the direction music had taken in his day. (J.S. Bach, Handel, Vivaldi, and one presumes a host of many others.) In his teaching he believed music, and specifically that for Church, had gone astray. He believed that the new developments were too instrumental, extreme and vulgar. Therefore, he felt, composers should go back to the way Palestrina composed. In his book, *Gradus ad Parnassum* (*Steps to Parnassus*), he advocated the teaching method known as Species Counterpoint. Other writers had anticipated this method, but Fux's book popularized it. Aside from a purely choral approach to rhythm that involved only whole, half, quarter and 8th notes in very basic groupings, his method reinforced the practice of thinking linearly in all voices. It downplayed the importance of chordal progressions, and especially the more adventurous progressions and modulations common in his day, the sort Vivaldi was using. So, in the midst of a sea of Baroque music filled with a joy of harmonic change, roulades of fast notes, singers imitating instruments and dramatic effects, this book truly went against the grain. Ironically, Fux's method caught on fast, and spread far and wide, proving to be a useful tool for teaching. As the Baroque period progressed, private instruction likewise proliferated. And, here was a book that guided teachers with beginning students. But, while there was certainly interest in learning to write for choral groups, there probably was not much interest in emulating Palestrina (to them, whomever that was). In its favor, the *Gradus*, seemed to rely on overriding linear truths that were above style. Those truths, involving basic lines, seem to be present in the music of the great composers of the Baroque, Classic and Romantic periods, and often in much 20th Century music. It amounted to hearing music in at least two simultaneous speeds.

Almost as soon as Fux's book spread, other teaching composers began adapting Fux's teaching method to their own purposes, often involving the instrumental way of composing. It certainly forced composers to think in a middle-ground way amid many speeding notes. Ironically, Baroque compositional methods, so abhorred by Fux, were already on the wane in his day. The new Preclassic methods, appearing first in the 1720s, emphasized the so-called Primary Triads I, IV and V. Even then Fux's method remained useful. Mozart employed it, and examples exist of his corrections on a student's work. Fux's Species Counterpoint never really stopped being used. For the next few centuries, newer adaptations of Fux would be changed and adapted to new ways of thinking, so much so that Twentieth-Century translations and reprints of the actual Fux book were a novelty in revealing what Fux had actually taught.

THE UNIQUENESS OF OCCIDENTAL HARMONY
Harmony on a grand scale had been developing in Europe during the Medieval and Renaissance periods. While music of other world cultures, then and now, could claim parallel existence, development, and growth in such areas as rhythm, melody and other dimensions and parameters, none could then, or now claim an equal status with European Harmony. It was and is unique. For the next few centuries "Theory" would concern itself primarily with Harmony. Here was an area about which aspiring musicians felt they knew the least. And if European Harmony was a growing dimension, it would only be a matter of time before a figure would appear with proposed answers to some basic questions. At the start of the 1700s, the situation was ripe for a major Theorist.

RAMEAU
Jean Philippe Rameau (1683 – 1764) and Johann Sebastian Bach (1685 – 1750) not only appear in Music History at the same time, but in time they would also complement one another in a significant way, though they had never met. One hypothesized, and the other, creating intuitively, demonstrated

the full breadth of those hypotheses in highly artistic examples. However, both, if at all, were only remotely aware of the each other. That Rameau also composed should be of no concern here because his music does not fully demonstrate nor test his theories to their fullest. When those theories are applied to the music of Bach, Rameau is shown to be overwhelmingly correct. Oddly, there seems to be a small gulf between what Rameau hypothesized, and what he composed. Certainly his scores were created intuitively, but they contain features that are not properly accounted for in his treatises. A major feature that separated the two was that Rameau was primarily a melodist, while Bach, a constant contrapuntist and the greatest Baroque harmonist (and perhaps of all time) presents an ocean of successful scores that invite harmonic analysis. Rameau's ideas are here put to the test. Many 20th Century Theory classes set out as their primary goal the more full understand of the harmonic progressions of J. S. Bach while using the postulates of Rameau. In keeping with that, the music Bach will here be occasionally mentioned.

While the music of J.S. Bach attracted limited attention during his lifetime, and while Fux's book on Species Counterpoint caught on among many private teachers, the technical thinking of composer Jean Philippe Rameau started dominating the Parisian music scene in the mid 1700s, and Paris was the cultural center of the world. What was discussed there was automatically international. Thus Rameau's first book was read throughout Europe by musicians and non-musicians alike. Among some spokesmen in the centuries that followed, Rameau was felt to be the "Prince of Theorists," and for good reason. (Here the pompous sounding label "Theorist" seems more appropriate because, in addition to help trace Root movement, he almost proved that harmony was a science based on overtone fact.) Eventually, and with the help of a French aristocrat and sponsor, Alexandre Poupliniere, Rameau would publish around twelve books over the next 40 of his 81-year life. That same patronage also enabled him to write and produce a series of important operas. France's sizeable aristocratic and bourgeois population was treated to one large Rameau stage production after another, thus increasing his importance as a composer. This all happened in the decades before the big revolution.

Rameau's first book, *Treatise on Harmony*, was published in 1723, and predated the Fux book by two or three years. Though the Rameau book quickly became fashionable for important musicians to read, it was not well written nor easily understood. In time others would step in and simplify Rameau's ideas for a more mass consumption. The most important of Rameau's early "translators" was Jean le Rond D'Alembert who was almost forty years younger. While among musicians the Rameau book was taken very seriously, it was the intellectuals in the Academy of Science who caused the biggest stir. The members believed that Rameau had proven, or was trying to prove that musical harmony was indeed a science, and that led to Rameau often being invited to assert himself, print replies, argue and interact with the Academy's membership, a number of whom were then, and would remain renowned. Maybe some of the members knew all along that music contained too many ingredients to ever be successfully explained in scientific terms, but any rationally objective explanation of any part of music, especially harmony, was a welcome subject.

However, it may be that Rameau's twelve books were largely aimed at an audience of working musicians who were creating music expertly, but who did not understand why or how harmony worked. Today, many of his statements have no validity unless measured against the norms and mindsets of the times, or in a particular musical situation that suited a particular statement. Rameau was affirmed by what he discovered in the overtone series found in typical windpipes and strings. Thus he claimed that triadic harmony and progression was natural because it is found in nature. But he dismissed other kinds of objects in nature that produced non-triadic overtones such as rods, disks, bells and plates. Whereas the music of his times was triadic, Rameau was only interested in finding overtone triads.

Rameau pointed out that the 1st, 2nd and 5th scale degrees are present in the major scale in the overtones of a single note. Moreover, in the Overtone Series of a single tone, one can determine an obvious Root and its triad. From that same Series are found inversions of the same triad, as well as certain other triads within a major scale. He was now dealing with the inversions of a triad. In merely speaking of these things in his books, other minds started arriving at other logical conclusions. Rameau had opened the door. Now it was possible to trace Root movement in a chordal phrase, and others even later would develop Roman numerals for chords on each scale degree. Rameau pointed out that from the lowest overtones one can determine the best next chord, hence chord successions dictated by "nature." Root movement by a 5th was very "natural." While such Root movement was common in the music of his day, until his discovery he had no scientific proof of why it was so satisfying to composers. He had hoped to prove how all the best progressions were indicated in the Overtone Series, but there he was halted. The use of IV was common in his and others of his time, but he was never able to show its existence in the Series. Also, he could not scientifically verify Root movement by 3rds, or the minor scale and its triads.

Other ideas also remained elusive. In successive books he would sometimes stumble into false leads, and that in turn led to other wrong premises, but the result of all the wavering was, on balance, ultimately positive. (In 1917 Scottish professor and author, Matthew Shirlaw called Rameau the most honest of Theorists because he frequently admitted when he was wrong.) All through Rameau's many stumblings, the French intellectual establishment enthusiastically took part, sometimes agreeing, and other times arguing. While the public discussions could get heated, all participants seemed to enjoy the exchanges because science and polemics were their province. Ultimately Rameau came out scarred, but right. But, no matter what scientific reasoning he gave for harmony, Rameau still insisted that music was a medium of sounds, rather than mathematical or scientific formulas. (In this he might be the greatest of empiricists.) So interested was Rameau in the basic triads of music that he dissociated himself from the contemporaneous Couperin melodic and ornate-type music, saying he was against the excessive decorations so fashionable in his day. He said very little about melody of any kind, other than that it arose from harmony.

RELATIVITY OF DISSONANCE
A further development during the Baroque period was the emergence of contextual consonance. Whereas the composers of the Renaissance knew exactly what dissonance was, and treated it with restrictive rules, the Baroque composers treated the V^7 as if it were consonant. One could leap to or from any note in that chord with impunity. In context it sounded consonant, and therefore dissonance avoidance rules did not apply. This practice extended to any chord that could be of Dominant function, such as the so-called vii chords in various versions.

THE TEXTURAL RULE OF THREE
Somewhere in the development and growth of instrumental music composers happened upon the discovery that the typical listener can only perceive three independent textural continuums (bottom – middle – and top) happening simultaneously. The three-voice Fugue would satisfy that limitation. For instance, block chords would be just one textural voice. But, what about four or five-voice fugues? Composers, and especially J. Sebastian Bach would, at any given instant, link certain of the voices in such a way that the listener could attend to that limitation of three. It is interesting to trace instrumental textures in successful scores from the Baroque period and on to test this Rule of Three. Any deviations would be temporary, and perhaps for the limited effect of intended turmoil.

INVERTED CHORDS AND ROOT MOVEMENT
Perhaps the most important of Rameau's assertions, and it was not truly new by his day, was that the bass note was not always the most important note (the Root) of a chord. Chords could be "inverted" so that the Root could be somewhere above the bass. Earlier musicians, especially keyboardists, had always wanted to know more about successful chord progressions. They could hear them sounding proper, but why? Up until Rameau, they were dealing with alleged simplifications that involved myriad chords. There was a need for some overriding principle. Rameau subsequently supplied them with a clearer way of dealing with the matter. His method was highly logical and reduced the vast number of established chordal progressions into clearer headings.

It would not serve us well to recount all the claims, and false leads that Rameau experienced and wrote about. (Matthew Shirlaw's 1917 book, *The Theory of Harmony* does so.) Rameau kept expecting to find ever more ultimate musical truths in the overtone series, and that quest bogged him down. Always thinking of his prestigious audience of scholars and intellectuals, he seemed bent on proving that the overtone series offered yet more guidance for good progressions. On that and other points he would often trip. The timeless music of J.S. Bach, appearing in Rameau's day sometimes verify Rameau's claims, and at other times contradict them. Rameau acknowledged that Root movement by 2nd and 3rd did exist, but they were not as good as Root movement by 5th, because the latter was so plainly evident in the Overtone Series.   While he easily proved the overtone validity of the major triad and most of the major scale, his troubles and vacillations involved the origin of the subdominant scale degree, the origin of the minor triad and minor scale, the relationship of major to minor, and the positive effect of Root movement by a third. An outstanding anomaly in Rameau's thinking involved what we would later call IV resolving to V. By his thinking it should not happen. Yet, in his own, and in most music of his day there were frequent the IV – V – I progressions and cadences.

THE RESULTING THIRD (simultaneous) NUMERICAL SYSTEM

A rock-solid contribution of Rameau, though others would refine it, was clearer thinking involving triadic chordal members. Without realizing it, he brought about a third simultaneous numerical system that helped to plot and analyze harmony. Though he was not thinking in terms of three systems, the outcome was clear. His Theory of Inversion, while not completely new in his day, said officially to all musicians that triads had Roots, 3rds, 5ths, and often 7ths. To demonstrate all three simultaneous numerical systems, let us imagine what we would call a V^6. The note that is a 3 above the bass is simultaneously the 2nd degree of the scale, and the 5th of the triad. Now this would present a temporary, slight complication to teachers and learners attempting to think Theoretically. But its value would prove itself.   All three numerical systems would simultaneously disagree when Inversions were involved. Even in todays Triadic Harmony classes, that point presents a preliminary hurdle.

TYPES OF CHORDS

Rameau rejected the so-called Double Perfection, a "thirdless" hollow-sounding octave with a perfect 5th at a cadences. In reality that practice was slowly dying throughout the 1600s. And by Rameau's early years, it could only be rarely heard. Rameau said that, since chords are generated by stacking thirds, harmony should involve full triads and some Seventh chords. The Mm was the most perfect 7th chord because it is plainly in the Overtone Series. All other chords, so-called "tall" chords, are derived from triads and 7th chords. Penultimate, and antepenultimate chords in phrases have a special need for 7ths. He rejected Augmented and diminished triads for not being fundamental because they lack the necessary perfect 5th. He also said that the stacked thirds should not rise higher than an octave. Thus "tall" 9th, 11th and 13th, chords are derived from their triads and 7th chord foundations, and should not be thought of as chordal entities.   The seventh chords Rameau accepted would be (in our nomenclature) the MM, Mm, mm, dm, and dd. He rejected other possible types because they were not in the overtone series. According to Rameau, the dd 7th chord is derived from the Mm with its Root raised a minor 2nd. For hundreds of years after Rameau, Harmony writers and teachers did indeed accept the tall chords as entities. They adapted Rameau's original claims and stacked thirds to suit their often convincing chordal explanations. Going any farther into Rameau's 7th chord reasoning proves counterproductive, since some of his logic in the long run proved fruitless. However, he did help to put his followers on the right track. So ultimately, notions of 9th, 11th and 13th chords really owe their origin to Rameau's concepts. He is further vindicated in that, the use of tall chords in successful later scores, seems to verify that they should be used as one would use their foundation triads and 7th chords.   He never mentioned what later Theorists would call Augmented 6th chords. In fact, he does not recognize that chords can come about through the movement of voices. He probably regarded them, as did the many composers of his time, as nothing more than mere voice movement. He did, however, acknowledge the existence of I^9, IV^9 and V^9 (of course, derived from triads).   And he had a rationale for Tonic 11th chords that approximates the 20th Century teaching that it is a dominant function.

Remember that Rameau was not telling people how to compose, but rather describing how the successful music of his day worked. In his experiments he never found his long-sought-after supreme principle for chord formation, other than just stacking thirds. Nor could he prove that all chords come from the Overtone Series. But he did assert certain important principles: What we would later call, I, IV and V were the basic triads. The tonic is the chord of repose, and it has no need to resolve anywhere. He also did not conceive of (what we would call Predominant function ii's and IVs,) and how they functioned in phrases. His music demonstrated that principle, but he had not rationalized it. That would remain for his followers. And remember that he did not think in terms of Roman numerals, even though his writings made them possible later on. Every chord but the tonic must be regarded as dissonant, or potentially so. This challenges modern definitions of dissonance. For instance: We want to hear the tonic triad, and therefore a ii triad is not that, and hence is dissonant. To make a triad sound as if it were a tonic, one should have nearby a triad whose Root is a perfect 5th above it (the Dominant), and another nearby triad with its Root a perfect 5th under it (the Subdominant). When the Root dropped by a perfect 4th, he labeled that as an Irregular Cadence. What we would later call Plagal and Authentic Half Cadences were for him necessary but Irregular. He knew that they sounded less affirmative. Oddly, he did not think clearly concerning Tonic chord consistency throughout a piece. But he was aware the listener could remember the sound of the Tonic chord.

Rameau's insistence that I, IV and V were the basic triads may have been a major contributor to the musical styles to overlap and follow the Baroque period, the Preclassic and Classic. The so-called Preclassic music, so filled with I, IV and V, began appearing in the same decade of Rameau's first book. Neoclassic and Classic composers rejected most adventurous harmony in favor of the three basic triads.

WEIGHTY POSTULATES
According to Rameau, melody has its origin in harmony, and harmony guides it. (This opened a never-ending argument that first comes melody, which then leads to harmony.) Scales arrive from the subconscious (not his word) perception of overtones. Overtones also similarly supply the Fundamental Bass and guide towards correct progressions. Rameau claimed that the minor mode or scale is really a variation of the parallel major scale. Compared to the major, it is imperfect. However, he was unable to explain much else about minor triads or minor keys. The Overtone Series was of no use on those points.

FUNDAMENTAL BASS
        (Best thought of as natural chordal change, and sometimes called Thoroughbass)

The V – I was the only progression that Rameau could prove with overtones. But since he had found the perfect 5th low in the Series, it proved to him how "fundamental" it was for chordal movement. Therefore naturalness of the perfect 5th made possible his theory of the Fundamental Bass. It is a bass line that is either rising or falling in perfect 4ths or 5ths. The major mode can thus be constructed (and harmonized) from a fundamental bass notes Roots that move by perfect 4th or 5th. Therefore Rameau advocated Root movement by those intervals as much as possible.

While Rameau failed to prove satisfactorily his Theory of Fundamental Bass, his writings helped composers to regard harmonic progression as not merely a matter of random choice. There is such a thing as the perfect progression, or resolution. Allowing for some Root movement by 2nd and 3rd, successful progressions should move mainly by perfect 5th and sometimes by perfect 4th. But, Rameau the Theorist could contradict Rameau the composer. For instance, (and here using nomenclature he did not use) the IV chord should not resolve to the V. Yet, that progression regularly recurs in his music, prominently at cadences. What made sense to his ear conflicted with some of his laboratory findings and assertions.

Root movement by 5th had been in effect well before Rameau's official endorsement. By the end of the 1600s the major/minor scale system was the norm, and fixed chordal progressions had evolved to reinforce a key, a key being the new sense of tonality focused on a home triad. It is difficult to cite specific scores and dates, but by 1699 Root movement by 5th and the V – I resolution had been well established. Triads were progressing so as to assure which chord was the Tonic. There was also the so-called Structural Cadence, I – IV – V – I . Formulation of that structural device took place in Germany. J. S. Bach was 14 years old in 1699, and then was consistently using I – IV – V – I cadences and progressions, and he continued doing so for the two decades before Rameau's first book. The same cadence/progression was also in the music of many of Bach's German contemporaries. But to understand Rameau here, we must remember that he was describing the mechanics of what he heard, and why some music worked well and other music did not. In his Theory of Fundamental Bass with Roots moving mainly by perfect 5^{ths}, Rameau also puts forth his innovative premise of Roots by Supposition (or by inference). That means listeners can hear a bass note that is not sounded. This is Rameau being highly perceptive. Such a premise helps to explain a number of satisfying harmonic moves that would otherwise beg for a Rameau-oriented explanation.

RAMEAU SOLECISMS

Rameau, in explaining progressions within a given piece, seems to think in little islands of progressions, rather than one overriding key. For him familiar progressions tonicize a local chord, and that can happen in different instances, irrespective of what we would call the main tonic. Tonicizing takes place if a chord nearby has a Root a 5th under, and another with a Root a 5th over. Yet, he says this without acknowledging what was in his and other music: the increasingly present Structural cadence/progression. Penultimate chords in phrases should include dissonance (what we would call a 7th) so that they will not be mistaken for the tonic.

SOLID RAMEAU LEGACY

Rameau found what we would call the dominant seventh chord in the overtone series, thereby affirming its seemingly appropriate and frequent use. Bach and Rameau seem to differ regarding what the 20th Century Theorists would call a vii $^{dim.6}$. Rameau reasoning says that it is really a V7 without the Root being sounded. Rameau allows for what he calls Root by Supposition, in other words Roots mentally, but not physically heard. In Rameau's time and long after, chordal 7^{ths} properly resolve down by step. (However, J. S. Bach does treat the vii$^{dim.6}$ triad as a separate triad, and what Rameau would call the 7th easily resolves up in Bach's music.) Also, for Rameau, and in his own language, a IV triad with an added 6th above the bass remains a IV triad, and not a ii$^{6/5}$. Or, at least, Rameau recommended a double analysis. (Regarding it as a IV would be contested by many 19th and 20th Century Theory writers and Teachers. Consistency, for them, dictates that stacking of thirds holds for all chords in determining Roots.)

Rameau's notion of the Fundamental Bass, while not clearly described, nor clearly understood, resulted in succeeding generations of composers looking for natural sounding progressions, frequently relying on Root movement by a 5th. He also induced succeeding generations of musical specialists to look in the overtone series to explain certain scales, intervals and chords. His claim of Roots by "supposition," is intriguing and not easily dismissed. (Such as diminished triads implying a bass note that is not physically heard, but mentally supplied by the listener.)

Rameau said very little about counterpoint, rhythm and meter, and he seemed to downplay nonharmonic tones. Suspensions were mentioned only in terms of certain chordal notes. As mentioned above, he claimed that melody arises from harmony. In fact, he said, one can hear melodic 2nds from the overtones of a V – I progression. The first time he referred to overtones as "harmonics" was in 1737. He was ahead of his time in defining closely related keys. Whereas, back then, and even today in harmony classes, a closely related key has either the same key signature, or one accidental away. He, on the other hand claimed that a closely relate key, chord or modulation existed when the tonics of the old and new chords form a consonant interval. At its most radical this premise meant, for instance, that C major and A flat major were closely related. It is a principle that allows for modulation by chromatic third – so typical of Romantic era music in the 1800s. However, a century after Rameau gave his notion of close key relationships, harmony teachers were still disagreeing with him.

RAMEAU'S SIGNIFICANCE

It may be that Rameau's significance really lies in having put Theorists on the right track. Many generations of succeeding thinkers and teachers would take the principle of stacking thirds to new and sometimes highly personal interpretations. Also, while we could easily assume that Rameau had a mental template involving Roman Numerals I, ii, iii, IV, V, vi and vii, that assumption would be a wrong. As reiterated above, he did not think in Roman numerals. To him there was no existence of a iii or vi. Instead, by identifying Roots of triads, followers were then enabled to put a potential Root on each scale degree, and that led to Roman numerals signifying seven triads in the key. That, in turn would lead to the labeling and classification of progressions. (Progressions that had been intuitively arrived at earlier.)

Odd though it may seem, he was additionally myopic in other harmonic matters. He claimed that music was just a succession of cadences. He was plainly not thinking of the total succession of chords, choral functions and an overall tonic. Instead, it seems that most of his claims involved just two or three chord units. If he created or located a favored chord change involving perhaps a Root movement by a 5th, he might easily call the second chord a Tonic, irrespective what it would seem when the overall key is taken into account. To us that chord might be a ii, but to him it was a tonic to prove his particular conclusion concerning Root movement. However, even with this questionable practice, he struck upon certain truths that put later followers on the right track. It would be up to successors to fill in the details and create a greater consistency of tonality and Roman numerals. Rameau remained vague about the significance of the Fundamental Bass, and about Roots that move by 3rd.

It took Rameau a long time to crystalize the concept and label of what we call a Supertonic triad because he had clung to his I – IV – V principle. To us, a ii triad, later called a Supertonic chord, would fit nicely into his system of Root movements by 5th, but he resisted that realization for quite a while.

CRITICISMS OF RAMEAU

As indicated earlier, Rameau had contemporary critics. Since he had claimed that Harmony was a Science, that claim opened the door for self-styled scientists to want more proof. But, aside from certain Overtone basics, Rameau could prove little else. After he died, the criticisms continued over such things as Rameau's indifference to the odd overtone produced by bells, plates, etc. Were they not "natural" too, just as much as a triad? One critic pointed out that if perfect intervals had a pure ring, and imperfect intervals (3rds and 6ths included) produced beats, "natural" music should therefore only involve perfect intervals. In reality music was using "unnatural" intervals, thereby not being very scientific. One hundred years after Rameau, the respected Theorist Hugo Riemann faulted Rameau for not saying that Harmony was empiric, thus the result of experience and taste, as well as overtones. But it may be that Rameau had already hinted at that. Almost contemporary with Riemann was Prof. Matthew Shirlaw (mentioned earlier), one of Rameau's ardent devotees, who, in agreeing with Rameau, warned that Harmony cannot be completely empiric/arbitrary. He also faulted Rameau for implying that the Mm 7th chord was consonant because it was in the Overtone Series, when it clearly is dissonant. Shirlaw also wondered just how Melody arises from Harmony. He also joined in the growing complaint of Rameau having very little to say about meter and rhythm. Perhaps Rameau was probably just taking rhythm for granted. Any technical observer of music would know that since the 1400s, dissonances were usually employed in weaker metric positions. Why would he, Rameau, need to point that out?

Theorist Giuseppe Tartini in 1754 may have been the first, in his writing to take the Rameau ideas he liked, and blend them with his own. He, too, liked proving certain things with overtones, and that harmony, and by extension Music (to him) was indeed a Science. No one seemed to point out the inconsistency of this conclusion. Whatever Tartini's methods, he seemed to find going from IV to V acceptable, even though Rameau, at least in his Theoretical writings, did not.

APPROPRIATE CONCERNS

Rameau had started a trend whereby would-be-musician/scientists, in makeshift laboratories, were trying to prove various points through tunings and overtones. But perhaps that issue leads to a dead end. Acoustical facts found in the lab (combination tones, the arithmetic versus the harmonic division of the octave, and on, and on) would at best furnish music with usable sonic concepts, and no more. How those sounds fit into music would be the musician's role. Real progress in understanding music depended on whether the finished product succeeded with listeners. By the late 1800s the concept of Psychology come about, and it, too, would be of little help in explaining music to creative musicians. It would merely reiterate what successful composers, before and after Rameau, were dealing with: That teachers and pupils of music were almost exclusively concerned with how to move notes around a on a staff, and how audiences would react, rather than how any particular chord proved itself in nature. They were concerned with perceived consonance, dissonance, and apt, poignant and memorable musical statements.

So, it follows that a proper history of written music ideation up to our modern times should discount phenomena found in the lab and concentrate on successful scores, as well as the practices and rules that guided our best composers, teachers and pupils. And to answer the question put by Matthew Shirlaw in 1917, "Where do music sounds come from?" The answer is that most come from that vast uncharted territory, the human mind. Let us deal with the notes themselves. Rameau and his followers would point out acoustically superior and inferior sounds, and it was always up to composers to weave them into perceived pleasing statements. It may be that examining the harmonic practices of J.S. Bach is a good beginning, since he was acclaimed to be the father of an entire succeeding era by the great composers who followed him.

Chapter 9 THE TRIUMPH OF INSTRUMENTAL MUSIC
(From here on the word Theory usually refers to methods and rules of writing music.)

By the early 1700s figured basses (or Thoroughbass) would lead to tonic-affirming acceptable chords and progressions that were increasingly being used. And, sometime in the first half of the 1700s, by common consensus, the duration dot, so common to the Renaissance, would be increased to a double dot. After its appearance around 1725, the Fux method of Species Counterpoint helped teachers to create SATB scores that respected the four human voice ranges, minimized leaping, while used passing tones, neighbors and suspensions in their proper metric positions. In Fux Harmonic progressions were not part of the picture. Succeeding composer/teachers would also invent their own "Fux approach" so as to accommodate the major/minor systems of tonality. Many respected teachers were using figured bass exercises in teaching harmony, and that often meant thinking and writing instrumentally. By the mid 1700s, for a pupil to study with a Baroque oriented teacher meant studies in harmony. To study with a more modern teacher at that time meant concentrating on melody and the Rameau-prescribed basic triads. By the end of the century, opera was increasingly present, and hence there were teachers who specialized in the solo voice and dramatic/theatrical techniques.

Writing in 1746, English Theorist George Andrus Sorge, made occasional statements that pointed to the future: There are four triads, d, m, M and A. Triads can be formed on every scale degree. The diminished triad is half consonant. 6/4 chords are not obviously dissonant. He inconsistently recognized the use and importance of what we would call a Dominant 9th and minor 9th chords. He agreed that what we would call vii $^{dim.7}$ triad is a Dominant Seventh chord with a missing Root. He liked the Telemann 11th chord which he called a "Tower" chord. (Stacking that many thirds might easily seem like a tower.) Without knowing it, he agreed with Rameau that chordal 7ths need not be prepared and resolved as suspensions. He speaks as 7ths of chords normally being passing tones. In his own way he speaks of the V7 as a contextual consonance. The generation of J.S. Bach had been treating that chord as an acceptable consonance since the late 1600s. And it continued as a common practice in the 1700 and 1800s. In summary: Whereas Renaissance composers would never use just any size 7th as if it were consonant, Baroque composers by 1699 regarded the V7 as a perfectly acceptable consonant chord, provided there was a resolution to the Tonic. And they did so without thinking in terms of later common labels or nomenclature. J.S. Bach's extensive counterpoint has chordal 7ths sometimes resolving as freely as the triadic notes.

Around 1755, Theorist Joseph Riepel wrote of chord hierarchy as related to the tonic. (This had already been in prominent music scores for the previous sixty or so years.) Though his writings are unclear on this matter, he at least opened the discussion. Around 1757, Theorist Friedrich W. Marpurg, who had once interviewed S. J. Bach, created a highly influential book that was used in a number of countries. He was concerned with the actual practice of music, and called his the Rameau/Marpurg system. Marpurg was among those few who published a set of rules for writing music. He said one should deduce important rules from what sounds right and is frequently used. Chords and intervals should be assembled from scales. Varieties of chords are created by combining various thirds. While 9th, 11th and 13th chords are possible, only the 9th chord has much use. And though they had come about by the movement of voices, he conferred chordal status to what would later be called augmented 6th chords. Without making a clear list of labels, he identified the five most closely related keys. (The music in Marpurg's day proves that closely related keys either had the same key signature, or were one accidental away.) The use of chords in the music of J.S. Bach confirms Marpurg's chord classifications.

JOHN PHILLIP KIRNBERGER
In his early days Kirnberger had been a pupil of J. S. Bach. Kirnberger had been listening to music and determining various functions. He endorsed the notion that all chords were stacked 3rds, but he did not go beyond the 7th chord. His 1770s, explanations of dd, 11th and 13th chords would in some respects agree with 20th Century explanations. He agreed with Rameau on the issue of Roots that could be absent from the chord, but supplied mentally by the listener. (For instance the vii06 is really

a V7) Kirnberger speaks of upper components in tall chords consisting of four notes. This suggests that he acknowledged a difference between an abstract chord with all five to eight pitches notes present, versus the actual usage where some notes in four-voice writing had to be omitted. (20th Century Thinkers, observing successful scores, would speak more clearly of tall-chord notes that can be omitted when composing in four-voices and other situations.) And typical of the growing attitude, Kernberger eschewed the lab, refusing to acoustically demonstrate where any of his scales, intervals, chords and scalar 7ths came from. His principles can be summarized.

In the V7 there are two leading tones of a different purpose. Together the 7th and 4th scale degrees create a vital tritone. A Leading Tone 7 remains an active tone and must resolve. (Leading Tones in iii chords are not part of his thinking.) However, in certain situations the 4th scale degree in a V7 can sometimes not resolve down by step. He calls I – IV - V Ground chords. He regards diminished chords (no doubt in First Inversion) as consonant. For him, the augmented triad does not exist. Do not stack thirds beyond 7ths. Seeming Chordal 9ths, 11ths and 13ths are the result of moving voices, and they must resolve before the chord changes. Seventh chords are essential, but not perfect. He regards what we would later call Predominant function chords as imperfect, as well as those that precede Predominant function. Chordal 7ths originally came about through passing motion, and they must resolve downward by step to another chord. Augmented 6ths are just the non-essential movement of voices that do not seriously change the original chord they are decorating.

Kirnberger thought that Rameau was too ready to declare a chord where there were merely passing notes. Unlike Rameau in his writings, Kirnberger accepted the commonly found ii6/5 resolving to a V. Like Theorists Heinichen, Mattheson and Sorge, Kirnbirger could not quite decide if the Second Inversion triad was consonant or dissonant.

MOVING ON
During the last phase of the 1700s, during the so-called Classical period, Theorists and teachers were relying on their own assembled and isolated facts, rules and procedures. They were probably not interested in a unifying theory or idea, but rather they were forming principles based on the music they found around them. They saw IV easily resolving to V, and ii6/5 was seen as a First Inversion ii7. They had no trouble accepting Roots that move by a 3rd and secondary triads (iii and vi). And in the face of the Primary Triads so constant in the Classical music of their day, they were unconcerned with any notions of extended Fundamental Bass.

In the early 1800s, the post-Rameau French, Italian and German Theorists added nothing new. Most of their unique points added nothing to the progress in understanding Harmony. In 1801, a decade after the start of the French Revolution, there was a Paris conference of eminent musicians and composers, Cherubini being the most famous. Those assembled were to decide the method of instruction at the Paris Conservatory. While realizing Rameau's enormous influence, they still officially abandoned his book, *The Theory of Harmony*, and instead they adopted the writings of C. S. Catel. Apparently Catel's book recycled certain Rameau principles, and mixed in practices and rules, long honored and common to the music of that day. For example: Avoid parallel perfect 5ths in any two voices, do not double any leading or other active tones, etc. Music of Catel's day would have included scores by Haydn, Mozart and Beethoven, as well as prominent others who enjoyed temporary fame. We must assume that the reason for having Theory on the curriculum was primarily to learn how to compose. There seemed to be no intent to dwell on historicism, other than to employ proven melodic and harmonic formulas. It is noteworthy that Beethoven studied instrumental technique with Haydn, and theatrical techniques with another composer.

At this point the motivation of the 1805 music-writing student should be taken into account. In the preceding decades, young people, usually men, approached prominent composers for private lessons. There may even have been those who merely wanted to learn without wanting to be composers. The Composer/Teachers in turn, needing the money, would take on pupils, knowing most would not all be competitors. As we move into the 1800s, more and more amateur composers sought and received training in this new manifestation of Theory. The Composer/Teachers, whether they had created their own, or used someone else's book or pedagogy, were teaching rudiments. Without any notion of what Theory was or should be, that service apparently satisfied the students. And if any one of the students had the spark to become composers of note, it would be up to them to know how to weave what they had learned into their future scores. Rudiments for them served as surrogate training. They learned rules within an artificial notational stricture as a point of departure. Right or wrong, this evolved in people's minds as Music Theory.

A major voice in Music Theory during the first half of the 1800s was that of the Belgian Francios-Joseph Fetis. He probably reflected the feelings of most musicians and composers at this time in rejecting pretense towards Science. There would be no numbers, proportions, and Overtone assertions. The answers for him would be in what he called the law of Tonality. (Vaguely put, it means that all chords circle and ultimately resolve to the Tonic chord.) Principles he regarded as crystal clear, were deemed by others to be vague and arbitrary. He claimed that once we had the major scale that then made possible the development of Harmony. A half-century later, Scottish professor Matthew Shirlaw would point out that Fetis was wrong in this point because back in the 1400s it was Harmony that first came about, and that had led to the major scale. Therefore the major scale had not always existed. But, in contradicting Fetis on an unsolvable polemic, maybe Shirlaw himself went too far by asserting that singers until the 1400s sang in Pythagorean tunings.

As the 1820s and '30s transpired, Fetis went on with his rules for writing music. Again, certain Rameau principles were incorporated, but Rameau's vague principle of Fundamental bass would be ignored. Rules: I, IV and V, because of their scalar Roots, were proper cadencing chords. Those chords should be in Root Position. All cadencing chords should have a Perfect 5th in them. The chief chords in music for Fetis were the major, minor and the Dominant 7th. In the case of the latter, Fetis welcomed Rameau's earlier discovery of it in the Overtone Series. Fetis had very little to say about the minor tonality, or about specific chordal progressions that circle the Tonic chord. The tritone in the V7, Fetis said, can be used as a consonance on its way to the Tonic chord. (J.S. Bach and his generation, well before Fetis, had already treated the full V7 as acceptable consonance. The minor 7th in a V7 needed no preparation. By Bach's day we have a new unspoken notion of contextual consonance. Beethoven had started his First Symphony with a V7 some twenty years before Fetis' writings.)

In 1853 Theorist Moritz Hauptmann likewise dismissed acoustics and scientific measurements as a basis for a theory of Harmony. Amid some eccentric reasoning, he made some interesting points: Everything proceeds from a major triad. The minor triad is a linearly inverted major triad. (Earlier said by Rameau and Tartini.) Hauptmann claimed that written music touches us metaphysically. In addition to I, IV and V, iii and vi are necessary. He rejected 11th and 13th chords as harmonic entities. In addition to accepting the usual chord progressions of his predecessors, he advocated chordal successions based on common tones. (This practice would appear in scores by the major composers of Hauptmann's century.)

Sooner or later a German interested in both Science and Music would enter the picture, and it happened in the person of Physicist/Professor Hermann von Helmlolz, a contemporary of Hauptmann's. (In the 20th Century Helmholz's work would ordinarily be regarded as Psychology.) In the 1860s he published several books, one being the *Theory of Music*, and another *The Sensations of Tone*. He was concerned with the physiological basis of human perception. He claimed the human has a need for some dissonance in music. His writings use the expression Klang. To him, a Klang was a combination of over- and under-tones. (Here he gets close to Rameau's findings.) Aside from his scientific commentary, Helmholz is only sometimes unique: A minor triad was an out-of-tune major triad, the 3rd of a minor triad is really the Root, also, the minor triad has a dual Klang. Since he was relying on Pseudo-Science for his reasoning, Helmholz left unaddressed a number of the familiar questions that had plagued his pseudo-Scientific predecessors: How do various scale degrees relate to the Tonic? Is there an acoustical basis for the minor scale? How do chords relate to the Tonic? What about IV going to V? What about chord successions that relate to the Tonic? "Klang" concepts would be taken further in the writings of Hugo Riemann.

In the second half of the 1800s Alfred Day was a major British Theorist, and, according to Shirlaw, his writings were influential. Amid his pseudo-Scientific findings, convoluted reasoning and rules, he devised explanations that were of little use in the progress of Music instruction. However, he did try exploring the upper partials of the Overtone Series in order to justify certain chords. Shirlaw, in 1917 said that Day's so-called discords were not found in real music. And, like everyone else, Day had no acoustical explanation for the minor triad.

Day was succeeded by four other British Theorists, some who advanced Day's ideas, such as they were. George. A. Macfarren, writing in 1860, claimed that the music of his day used unprepared dissonance. He cited isolated examples from as far back as Jean Mouton around 1550. John Stainer, writing in 1871, was more independent. He endorsed the tempered scale (still occasionally questioned), and in his own way he explained such things as a V13th in four voices as an example of omitted notes. He also attempted explaining augmented 6th chords in too technical a manner. Maybe Stainer is another in a string of Theorists fruitlessly looking for the small formula that explains all of Harmony. For example: The third might be the basis of all Harmony. The irony of all this is the kind of radically new Harmony combining thirds in new ways being created by Debussy and Ravel not too long after these statements.

By the 1890s Ebenizer Prout had tried building on Day's sometimes flawed pseudo-scientific explanations of chords. Then in 1903 Prout abandoned acoustics and science altogether in favor of harmony arising from Esthetic sensibilities. Like Albrechtsberger, and other Theorist/Teachers back in 1700s, Prout decided to assemble a list of practical facts and rules in teaching Harmony. A sampling of the Prout "rules" reveals little that was new. In 1917 Shirlaw objected to Prout using the word Theory in referring to something that was not founded on acoustical/ scientific findings. Esthetic reasoning, Shirlaw felt, was insufficient. But, like it or not, the expression Music Theory had been assuming a new connotation for some time. For many musicians, moving notes around to recreate stylistic or historic music accurately was grounds enough for labeling such books as Music Theory.

It would be wrong to ignore Theory/Composition training taking place in Germany all through the 1800s, and especially late in the century. In addition to private instruction by self-enterprising teachers, there was the newly opened Leipzig conservatory that attracted students from all over Europe, Edvard Grieg being one. In time German training would attract even some Americans wishing to know how to write music in the latest approved manner. It is an open question what pedagogies, if any, were used. A product of German training at this time would be Edward MacDowell. It is also noteworthy pointing out the kind of music he was writing after returning to New York from his German studies. While the writing is safely correct and even charming, it certainly does not reflect any of the dynamic new changes taking place in European scores at that time.

HUGO REIMANN

Perhaps the writings of German Theorist Hugo Riemann (1872 – 1919) represent a culmination of innovative thinking in major/minor tonal music. His is the voice of a stylistic era that was ending, his final book coming out in 1909. Riemann based Music on human perception, and he used self-observation to arrive at conclusions. In this matter he resembles a Psychologist. But, as a self-defined scientist, he would rely on acoustics, and some of his findings have proven erroneous. When it came to Music Theory, he never based his findings based on the creation of scores since he was not a composer. Had he been one, his writings would have had more impact. In classroom Theory he added very little that was new. To his credit he was interested in the History of Music Theory, and was probably the first to publish such a text (1898).

To Riemann, a Klang is a resonating sound with the usual overtones. But would the "Klang" be the answer to all questions? To aspiring musicians looking for guidance in creating music, Riemann's pseudo-Scientific explanations and Klang designations seem pretentious and useless. For instance his notion of six Klangs within a key is no improvement over the increasingly prevalent practice of Roman numerals I through vi. So, to music makers, most of his innovative claims went nowhere. There are, however, occasional points that prove minimally interesting.

Whereas major triads are found in the Overtone Series, he deduced that minor triads come from undertones. He explained the minor triad as a perceived sensation. Compared to Rameau's claim that there could be many tonics in a single piece, to Riemann there was only one tonic. Music moves from and to a single Tonic chord. While Riemann describes (what we would call) ii, iii, and vi as parallel Klangs, he does not go as far as telling the reader that he means they can stand in for the primary triads. Here we have an implied, but perhaps an unintended theory of substitute chords. Going on: For him, and succeeding teachers, 7ths, 9ths, and 13ths, when added to triads, do not change main function of the underlying triad.

Riemann also wanted symbols for chord functions -- not Roman numerals, but symbols that indicate importance or function of the chords in a phrase. His "LT" symbol means a Leading Tone change chord. (He makes no allowance for the occasional iii chord that has a Leading Tone in it. However, his LT designation proved useful. The later writings of Heinrich Schenker seem to recycle this line of thinking.) He recognized Secondary Dominants, and assigned them the symbol D. For all practical purposes his "P" seems to mean a substitute chord, a stand-in for one of the Primary Triads. (Still, his connection between parallel Klangs and substitute chords is not clear.) He advocated triadic progressions with common-tones. That sort of progression had been increasingly used in scores of the major composers throughout the 1800s. During a piece, Riemann says, if one is not hearing the tonic chord, there is a state of unrest – a sort of dissonance. In that sense all triads except the Tonic are dissonant. And in keeping with the future writings of Paul Hindemith, all twelve chromatic tones are related to the tonic.

Chapter 10 THE 20th CENTURY DICHOTOMY
TRADITIONAL THEORY CONTINUES WHILE MUSIC CHANGES

INCREASE IN STUDENTS AND SCHOOLS

In addition to Conservatories and undocumented private instruction, there was an increase in the number of Music Schools and Departments as the century progressed. Each institution had curriculum plans that required Traditional Theory. There were also a growing number of music specializations, major areas of study, that all required at least the lower levels of Theory instruction. In time the growing numbers of students needing Theory instruction (and the lure of textbook profits) led to a number teachers creating their own Theory books, both for private instruction and classroom use. Such books were often little concerned with historicism (how Bach, or any other great composer composed), but rather, they incorporated rules and procedures learned from previous teachers, mixed in with each author's unique approach. That was not really bad. Each book was teaching a valued, albeit rarified subject, along with procedures: How to write music that sounded proper and dignified. Maybe most of these books were unduly aimed at choir loft music.

Students were studying an abstraction known as Traditional Theory. Exercises usually involved SATB texture, and the results could be correct but bland. But, before the reader concludes that this was unfortunate, be reminded that in order to teach numbers of simultaneous students how to write music, one has to begin somewhere, and the SATB starting point is perhaps the best way. In some books there were occasional rules that had little basis in the reality of acclaimed music, but even that is excusable if the students were learning basic note literacy and discipline. All this organized pedagogy served a useful purpose in that students were learning mechanics and labels that helped them to be "literate" musicians. Students were also required, to a limited extent, to hear and write down what they heard. It would remain for each individual student to reconcile at some later time what they had learned with the real world of concert/recital, and even popular music, and how famous individual composers differed from one another.

Training in classrooms required more specific terminology. At some point, perhaps by 1900 the Theory world had adopted terminology for each scale degree: Tonic, supertonic, mediant, subdominant, dominant, submediant, leading tone and subtonic. Triads on each of those degrees were represented with Roman numerals I through VII. Perhaps by the middle of the century lower case Numerals indicated minor triads, and other symbols were added near the numeral to indicate diminished or augmented triads. Symbols were also added to Roman numerals to indicate the different sized seventh chords. Different textbooks had variations on this symbol system. The ancient Guidonian scalar syllables continued to be used in sight singing, and it was further developed into full chromatic variants. (f examples: Di = a raised Do, or se = a lowered sol). Americans put "ti" on the seventh scale degree, while Europeans continued using "si."

It was probably during the 1800s that the world of music, and especially the printers, had clarified and refined, and sometimes even labeled things such as extensive C clef usage, fermatas, words that indicated tempo and character, slurs and articulations, dynamics, decoration labels, key spellings with many sharps and flats, character words, short-hand repeat symbols, gruppetto indications, various systems, and dynamics. Many of these had appeared in the earlier Baroque and Classic periods, but standardization took place in the 1800s. There were also areas of disagreement, and certainly inconsistencies. Simultaneously cadence labels (Authentic, Plagal, Incomplete) would probably have originated in books used at conservatories.

THE NEW DEFINITION OF THEORY ENDURES

It seems that there had always been two mind-sets of Theory among those who claimed expertise. There had to be a significant parting of the ways. Either it is the inquiry into laws from Nature and hearing, or it is the assemblage and teaching of rules from practice. For instance, and as mentioned earlier, Matthew Shirlaw, in his 1917 book, *The Theory of Harmony*, is seriously concerned with finding basic musical sounds in Nature. He occasionally asks, "Where do these sounds come from?"

He often praises Rameau, then seems to chide him when he, Rameau, cannot justify enough with acoustics. (It might be likened to criticizing scientists for not knowing the origin of Electricity. It is there, so we use it.)

Either Music is Scientifically explainable, or not. And so far, successful Music has very little that can be proven in the Physics laboratory. Therefore Composition, and by extension Theory has to involve human sensibilities and the seemingly arbitrary search for the beautiful: Esthetics. It involves taste and discretion. If there are any possible answers, they are to be found in examining recognized works of beauty. In this sense Music Theory is the collection of rules and traits found in works created by acclaimed great composers from the throughout history. If answers are sought in music from the past, then it is positive Historicism. Historicism obviously subscribes to THE GREAT COMPOSER PRINCIPLE, a principle rejected by those seeking to democratize past figures in music history. (Such thinking easily sees all human advances springing spontaneously from the population at large.) We will stay with our genius principle. The music of Palestrina is a good example. His contrapuntal methods can easily stand as a summary for all Renaissance counterpoint. While there were other, sometimes earlier composers and slightly different practices, Palestrina's methods stand as a good point of reference. His methods also illustrate a high degree of skill not easily mastered. Other great composers can serve well for Theory practices in later historic periods. First comes the piece of music, or a whole body of works, created by our stipulated great composer, followed by appreciation, followed by attempts to objectify traits that are exhibited. Those traits are then codified into exercises that are passed on to interested practitioners and students. If such works demonstrate any scientifically provable reasoning or principles, it is so much the better.

But by the late 20th Century there was disagreement as to why one studies Theory. In colleges and universities, among some students, and those who controlled curriculum, there was disagreement over why students were required to take Theory. Was it necessary so that the writing of music could be mastered? Certainly not all students wanted to write music. And even if they did, was Traditional Theory fulfilling that need amid the radical stylistic swings and changes throughout the 1900s? Was Theory study only to learn basic musicianship? Or, was Theory instruction necessary because all needed to understand and write or talk publicly about music? Was Theory necessary merely to train good teachers? Or, was it learned so all would perform or conduct better? Was it so that all might analyze music better? Or was Theory a basic service in the training of instrumental performers and conductors, so that they would understand music literacy better? One administrator was even heard saying that Theory was merely an activity, and that performing on instruments was the main focus. With these kinds of questions floating around, and if taken to extremes, Theory instruction could, and did take quite a battering beginning in the 1960s. Disagreement on these issues may even remain persistent up to the present. And, depending on the emphasis at each institution and the "major" being pursued, the depth of Theory instruction varied. Maybe all of the above expectations can be met if they are allowed to take place without undue emphasis. The better students will always be able to adapt what they have learned to other ways of thinking.

For sure Theory is not doing its job properly if it does not deal in some way with the practices of the great composers of the past (1700 to 1900). For now, that deliberately excludes the 20th Century, primarily because of the enormous audiences for the previous music. As far as fledgling composers are concerned, Theory should never be regarded as composition instruction in present practices. Could the present really be satisfactorily taught, seeing that rules of the present are not immediately obvious, especially in a cultural picture that changes so continually? For developing composers Theory, rather, is a source of notational mechanics, as well as surrogate training for whatever the fledgling creative composer would devise.

A PROMINENT EXAMPLE OF POSITIVE HISTORICISM
Against a backdrop of status quo Traditional Theory instruction an interesting project took place at the Eastman School of Music perhaps beginning in the 1930s. Under the guidance of Prof. Ervin Allen McHose, students assisted in statistical studies of the musical practices in the J.S. Bach chorales. Here was an acclaimed huge body of choral works by the most respected harmonist of the previous two

centuries. (Beethoven referred to him as an "ocean" of harmony.) Here would finally be some sort of objectivity in stating Theory rules. Questions were asked as to how often percentage-wise Bach wrote such and such a chord or maneuver. And if it occurred often enough, it was then grounds for a firm rule. These statistics then formed the basis for the McHose text. If Bach did such and such in his music, it was then worth emulating in classroom exercises. There was never any implication that this approach should rule out non-Bach-like practices. The McHose approach was certainly a better basis for validity than that presented in other contemporaneous Theory texts. Here was perhaps the first attempt to base Theory instruction on the works of an acclaimed musical genius. And, like the study of Palestrina's practices, other devices and musical moves could be measured against a point of reference.

The McHose initiative also led to discoveries concerning nonharmonic tones (moving usually in 8th notes) as well as other techniques. The Bach's Chorales demonstrate nonharmonic tones so expertly, that it is easy to forget that the underlying chordal progressions and transpositions show how he revolutionized harmony. Other contemporaneous Texts, thinking they were emulating Bach's practices, might easily prove inadequate when confronted with the Bach's actual chordal maneuvers underneath the distracting nonharmonic tones. The McHose project seemed to suggest that other text authors should update whatever rules they had been stating. The McHose project also revealed a number of other facets of Bach's writing that bear attention. An added, and distantly related point is that Bach may have been the first and certainly the highest profile composer to create instrumental music that could be rescored for other instruments. To him the relationships of the notes on the staves were the highest priority. And if done properly, lines would work successfully in any instrumental combination. He would even rearrange his previous works for new instrumentation. When he copied and arranged the music of his contemporaries, he seemed to be proving to himself how lacking in dynamism the actual notes were in relation to one another. Take away the orchestral coloring and see what is left.

In some instances the various personalized Theory books available throughout the 1900s could not agree on definitions of some nonharmonic tones. For instance, the word appoggiatura meant at least two different things in opposing texts. (Is it a leap to a dissonance then resolved by step? Or is it merely any on-the-beat (stressed/accented) dissonance that resolves by step.) Theory instruction had also grown to include certain other procedures and chords not sufficiently demonstrated in Bach's harmonizations, for instance Neapolitan and Augmented 6th chords. Thus some text authors observed their use in the music of Bach's followers, and they extrapolated rules for exercises in deliberately concentrated situations. This was a good move, and it meant adding other exercises with musical devices common to the Classic and Romantic periods. There could be an odd mix of good and bad in some books. A good example is the highly popular Piston Theory book. On one hand his explanations of Neapolitan and Augmented 6th chords remained exemplary, but on the other hand his explanations of nonharmonic tones resulted in disappointing, if not incompetent results.

BUILDING ON RAMEAU: Some speculative thoughts and other observations.
Though Rameau, in his overtone experiments, could never account for the IV triad, he had no qualms about using that chord in his music. The IV's existence (if it must be proven "scientifically") is probably more the result of mental psychology: man's ability to hear upside down. It is the mirror image of the tonic triad. Its ubiquitous use in the Structural Progressions and Cadences show how it can safely be used without usurping the importance of I. The ubiquitous progression is always IV – V – I, and never V – IV – I. (More on that below.) Rameau, in a roundabout way, proves that IV, if not handled carefully, could well make the Tonic triad sound as if it were a dominant to IV. So the proper way to use a IV is to make sure it precedes the V, or to add dissonant notes to it, and, above all, to decrease its appearances. The so-called Plagal Cadence (IV to I) should never occur internally in phrases, but rather only at final cadences, and only when the listener has by then heard the tonic chord unmistakably asserted. Throughout all of Bach's chorale harmonizations, one can find very few Plagal Cadences. Its "Amen" sound may be one of a few unique features of the 19th Century Hymn style, a style known for its home-spun practicality rather than for artistic taste.

THE STRUCTURAL PROGRESSION or CADENCE.

Sometime in the mid 20th Century Theory instructors finally realized that Tonal music, as exemplified by Bach, Mozart, Beethoven, Brahms and their contemporaries seemed to rely on this progression and cadence. Rameau had denied it in his treatises, but used it in his music. Great Art music featured **predominant function** chords (ii or IV), followed by **dominant** chords that then resolved to the Tonic chord. That fact was there all along, except that it needed to be codified and proven through score examination. Maybe the ii – V – I was the harmonic secret that unified a great swath of music history (1700 to 1900), having waited in plain sight for its discovery. While Sebastian Bach's contemporaries were discovering the V – I, in his earliest scores he was already continually demonstrating the Structural Progression.

EXERCISES CONTINUE WHILE REFLECTING FEW OF THE ADVANCES IN ACTUAL INSTRUMENTAL MUSIC.

It seems the great composers of the 1800s (Chopin, Schumann, Mendelssohn, Wagner, etc.), being quite occupied with their piano and orchestral innovations, did not write much choral music, and moreover did nothing daring in their few scores for that medium. So, their harmonic innovations did not appear in those few choral scores. One chief reason facing those four or other Romantics was that choral singers were/are limited in what they can hear and sing. Hence 1800s choral music remained harmonically routine. Any teacher of Theory, armed with such limited musical examples, could only aim their students in the direction of bland choral writing, brought about by the often arbitrary part-writing rules mentioned earlier. Evidently few complaints were heard. If any student wanted to ultimately create instrumental music, the SATB rules could only served as a point of departure. If students in the late l800s were lucky enough to hear concerts featuring the more daring orchestral works of Wagner, they could/would then use their talents to somehow write instrumental music that was more up to date harmonically, and with varying metrical divisional notes. Also, the late 1800s saw fugal counterpoint being taught in the Paris Conservatory, and that helped students somewhat in thinking instrumentally. It may have also been the first official attempt to mimic the instrumental music of Bach. Probably beginning in the late l800s wealthy American music students started going to Europe to study how to write concert music. Usually it meant going to Germany where there were many private instructors prepared to teach the most conservative of harmonic procedures. When those Americans returned home, they easily influenced official Theory instruction that favored maintained the status quo. Undoubtedly, at the time musical Americans wanted to be up-to-date with their imagined European Artistic superiors. After he returned to the USA, it took MacDowell quite a while to venture into mildly innovative composition.

As the 1900s began, various other Theory related subjects were coming about. Books were being written that dealt with the recurring forms to be found in Classic and Romantic music. This was an attempt to not only label and categorize formal types, but it also opened the way for analyzing specific pieces, not so much for the harmony used, but rather how melodic surface and digressive modulations helped create the form of famously successful Classical pieces and movements. This led to Form and Analysis instruction and classes. Another subject that was put into textbooks was J. S. Bach oriented Counterpoint, no doubt led by the Fugal studies mentioned above. The Paris Conservatory in the late l800s had placed a high value on being able to create Fugues. As J.S. Bach's works were becoming increasingly known and respected, it seemed logical to teach students to use his various linear techniques. Hence (18th Century) Counterpoint eventually became a standard Theory subject. Ironically, any examination of the late l800s student fugues at the end of the text used at the Paris Conservatory (reprints being available) reveals harmonic stasis. Nothing was taught that even approximated Bach's dynamic control of harmonic progressions.

THE LATE 1800'S MUSIC VERSUS THE EARLY 1900'S THEORY INSTRUCTION

So, as the 1900s progressed, Theory students, no matter what their career goals, were hearing more and more "Bach through Brahms/Wagner" music at public concerts, and later through recordings. Bach obviously sounds quite different from Wagner, but both share important traits. But if Theory faculty and students wished to be up to date in late 1800s Wagnerian period style, they were given only partial satisfaction. Simple melodic dictation and four-part choral harmony dictation and writing, using mostly quarter notes were the instructional norm in typical classrooms. Still quite a bit of information could be passed along in appropriate exercises. Apparently there was not much difference between 1901 Theory exercises from what was taught in the continental conservatories in the previous century.

OTHER SUBJECTS: An incomplete list.

RENAISSANCE COUNTERPOINT
Here we return to the Fux book from 1725 and its Renaissance aims mentioned earlier. By curriculum extension the Contrapuntal practices of the 1500s, and especially that of Palestrina, presented itself as a viable subject of study, especially since its procedures differed so markedly from that Traditional Theory exercises. Palestrina's style encapsulates the methods shown by a range of different 1500's composers, though some of the composers were remarkably individual in their practice. This style emphasizes diatonic lines that move through triadic sounds which themselves have no sense of progression. Some Post WWI scholars devised pedagogies that guided students in the highly strict Palestrina method. Perhaps the most stylistically accurate was that written by Knut Jeppesen. For Theory instruction here was another valid and quite scholarly subject. And here, once again, Theory students, who were/are fledgling composers, would learn abstract principles that could subtly apply to newer composition. Surrogate training in Theory classes is an undocumented reality. The establishment of this subject in the Theory curriculum bore with it the suggestion that Traditional Theory would be only one Theory subject to be learned, albeit a highly important one.

SPECIAL TOPICS
Theory in advanced or specialized curricular levels, also eventually evolved into the generalized versus the specialized singular study. Whereas generalized instruction provided rules and procedures that could be found in whole bodies of literature, Special Topics courses could deal with the work of specific composers, or with specific and unique situations. They probably first appeared in the 1920s and involved untangling the unique techniques of composers whose work avoided the tonal language used in standard repertory by outstanding Classic composers. Such studies would be under the aegis of Special Topics, and would serve well for graduate study in the increasing numbers of Music Departments at colleges and universities. Whereas books in Traditional Theory could claim relevancy in dealing with standard repertory, Special Topics could deal with, among other things, estimable music outside the standard repertory. This creates a bothersome situation: Theory study may indeed lose validity if it does not continue to explain a widely accepted body of repertory. Unique compositions and the study of them can indeed represent efforts that went, and will go nowhere in Music's long growth, development and continuity. Unfortunately Special Topics courses can lead to research that few will ever read, thus cluttering the libraries. Is the library to be the depository of uniquely singular items that benefit no one? How does that teach mankind? Individuals struggle to find meaning in life only when they deal with patterns.

It is a fact that most, if not all of the renowned 20th Century American composers (and probably the European ones as well) were products of Traditional Theory instruction. Evidently the creative muse of each was not unduly hindered.

CHAPTER 11 THE OTHER SIMULTANEOUS 20th CENTURY:
THE CHALLENGE OF NEW THEORY INSTRUCTION

As the new century began, some composers felt the triad was passé, and either limited or avoided its use. Certainly Tonality was regarded by many as a spent technique. A number of advanced guard composers would begin relying on an anchor tone or chord throughout a piece, while a few radical others would reject any obvious "anchoring." When it comes to dissonance, there would seemingly always be composers falling into three basic groupings: The mainstream, using a moderate amount of newer 20th Century techniques, those who insisted on filling their scores using mostly techniques from the earlier era -- often producing works subtly new, and those who utilize approaches that are radically new, such as aphorisms. (Musical gestures that are stated once.) The potential audience size would be predictably larger in the case of the first two of the above-mentioned groupings.

A NEW WAY TO USE TRIADS
In the 1890s, and during Riemann's life, a new way of using triads, unrelated to rules of TONALITY, appeared in the music of Eric Satie. While a tonic tone and chord would be maintained, major and minor triads of any tonal level, could succeed one another in a random manner. Such a method could almost be described as chordal successions. As in Renaissance triad usage, Theory class Roman numerals would here be useless. Choice of triads would, of course, be determined by the melodic/linear surface of the piece, but there would be no preordained chord hierarchy or resolutions, other than that necessitated by linear movement. 20th Century mainstream composers would often attempt such radically unrelated triad successions. But was this procedure new? It had already been used in the more adventurous madrigals of Gesualdo in the late 1500s. But here in 1900 the practice was appearing anew, and it would remain a feature in the music of many conservative composers of the 1900s, even those who deserted notions of an anchor note or chord in specific pieces. Such writing could easily be simulated in classroom assignments.

Part of the early 1900s was the emergence of the new aesthetic in modern music among small pockets of composers. Among the more radical thinkers there was an attempted iconoclastic destruction of the 1800s way of composing music, and especially involving avoiding the then seeming worship of Wagnerian Music Drama. Small segments of European society were increasingly exposed to highly dissonant music that seemed to have no rules. Artistic revolution and radical change were in the air. Maybe it is no coincidence that simultaneously the most powerful European nations were rushing into a senseless war against one another. Composers of a more moderate nature were adding newer elements to their music, but at a more controlled rate of change. To hear their music was to know that it was new, and could not have been composed in the 1800s. But, whatever the moderate composers innovated, it seemed timid when compared with the work of more radical innovators. For the first few decades the radical "fringe element" could be ignored. Against that backdrop, Theory instruction, with its seemingly bland and dated approach, was not going to go away. It was a safe haven of sensibility, with reasonable rules that produced a "polite" student music. Timeless music-writing points and skill were still learned.

One reaction against the past was a renewed interest in simultaneously independent voices: Counterpoint. The newer approach to composition would avoid the old chord changes, and especially the obvious V – I. Independent voices, if they related to any chords at all, would pass through newer progressions, and even newer chord structures. As the century unfolded there would even be another new concept, so-called Linear Counterpoint, where the voices would avoid any attempt at conveying a controlled harmonic picture. Since dissonance was now "in," there would be any number of dissonant "bumps" of voice against voice. Now listeners were supposed to be listening to the linear flow, and not for any harmonic sense, at least not in the old sense. Ironically, cautious composers had to be careful so as to not unwittingly stumbling into old resolutions and familiar tonal-picture implications.

Perhaps the most radical change was advocated by Arnold Schoenberg and his small pre-WW I Viennese circle. That group was intensely engrossed in creating a new Musical Art. Schoenberg believed that dissonance was now liberated, and he showed by example that a recurring motive enmeshed in a new non-triadic harmony could unify a short and starkly original piece. The motivic idea was not new, but the linear method and harmony were. The composer was to use intuition and taste to create short pieces that were tightly organized, with each piece stressing a chosen simultaneity (a new kind of harmony) of a few pitches that could be restated vertically and horizontally. (It would take a number of decades before enterprising analysts could explain in Set Theory just how Schoenberg's procedures could be understood or analyzed in a Theory class.) Schoenberg was thus advocating atonal procedures. While Schoenberg hated the label "atonal," he was certainly avoiding Tonality and its established ways. Schoenberg knew that he was treading new territory, for the finished pieces according to his direction taxed the attention of even his outer circle of followers, to say nothing of ordinary concertgoers. To other teachers, had they known about the new music, and had they wished to stay abreast, there seemed to be no answers. Certainly exercises and compositions exemplifying such new pieces would have to be short, for there seemed to be no way to justify extended forms. But from an overview, and to point out a weakness in this "new approach," Schoenberg and his followers did not take into account how listeners actually hear music. The listener, while hearing, is performing as well. Since this new music was not for ordinary listeners, Schoenberg in his early 1900s years fostered a series of chamber concerts that were almost "by invitation only."

Teachers of Theory had many pupils all during the first decades of the 20th Century, and the teachers usually cared little for the newer "experiments." The new dissonant music also brought about a reactionary label that referred to the older ways, and it is a label that is used throughout this book: Traditional Music Theory. It thrived on positive historicism. To study it was to learn the inner mechanics of music created from the time of J. S. Bach to that of Brahms/Wagner. And that was good enough reasoning for maintaining the old Theory Pedagogical ways. Besides, many wondered just how transient the newer dissonant ways would be. Would there ever be a sufficient audience for the radical works? So it seemed safe and sensible to just stay with the tried and true instruction of Tonality in major/minor music. (That view would remain throughout the 1900s.) After all, anyone could/can create dissonant note combinations, but how would the results be perceived and accepted as valid music, even to the few listeners attracted to it? To make matters more vivid, symphonic audiences were insatiable in their desire for late Romantic music, and the audiences were the largest they would ever be. There was a passionate support of a dimension that perhaps would never be matched again. That fervor for all kinds of concert music would be somewhat curtailed by the 1914-18 Great War. And as the 1920s unfolded music and its support endured an identity crisis because of a lost equilibrium.

Later, and throughout the 1900s it seemed as if concert audiences only wanted to hear the music from the 1800s. Those teaching theory, and creating new music curricula were faced with the dilemma of possibly throwing out instruction that related directly with the very 1800s music, a music that audiences and performers preferred, versus plunging into uncharted territory. And besides, what rules and guidelines were typical of the new music? In spite of that situation Traditional Theory survived because interest in the Bach through Brahms music never waned, even to the present. Any instruction that recognized and dealt with the newer dissonant techniques of the 20th Century would then have to be an adjunct to the Traditional pedagogy. However, since Theory instruction is charged with explaining the inner mechanics of music, it would be forced into a century-long chase after methods in the newer scores that seemed to change with each new composer and score, and that could be taught.

Compounding the 20th Century picture was the emergence of a parallel world of popular culture and its music. On its side would be the potential masses of humanity, easily won over by music they could understand and support. The world of highly literate, and seemingly exclusive concert/recital music would increasingly be marginalized as the century progressed.

In spite of a slowing down between the two World Wars, it was a century of many self-proclaimed compositional leaders and innovators who wanted to demonstrate their unique originality. In an egalitarian society there will always be more imagined than real "master minds." Just at the point when a certain method was mastered to the point of viable classroom presentation, ever new replacement techniques, sometimes contradictory, would come along thus confounding teachers and professors. This process seemed to peak in the 1960s. Often composers were attempting to create sonic "experiences" that had never been heard before. That in itself would present teaching problems. If ten hypothetical new works share nothing in common, how would that fit into the goals and procedures of classroom instruction? Music pedagogy depends upon showing common features in whole bodies of works, and not in dealing with solitary experiences. Another problem is one of aesthetic evaluation of scores. So as not to waste time on music that will not survive, how would any teacher know which scores to emphasize? To evaluate a new (somewhat or highly) dissonant work demands repeated hearings. In that respect the phonograph proved to be a valuable aid throughout the 1900s. If repeated hearings reveal nothing, then the only valid conclusion is that the piece is indeed vacuous and a waste of time. Here there is also the worry that "super listeners" might understand a realm not understood by more ordinary listeners.

TEACHING 20ᵗʰ CENTURY TECHNIQUES

After 1950 textbooks appeared that attempted to incorporate terminology and exercises involving the more basic elements of early 20ᵗʰ Century music. It was a welcome breakthrough when anything found in the scores of Stravinsky, Hindemith, Bartok and their contemporaries, could be turned into exercises. Naturally, those books and exercises would deal with the more conservative of innovations, but at least students were exposed to something closer to their time. However, the total picture of modern score realities and the distance from classroom instruction remained remote and quite complex.

BACKTRACKING:

To the potentially interested masses, harmony only meant triads, and they could not conceive of newly structured harmonic effects that deliberately used sharply dissonance chordal constructions. To them, the new sounds all seemed too alien and anarchic. However, WWI seemed to cause a huge cultural shift, and an abatement of any notions of a new supposedly revolutionary music. Even those creating and preferring traditional music were undergoing an adjustment. After WW I, and while the tonal "revolution" went underground, mainstream music adopted certain milder changes, such as Jazz influences and Classical score emulation. The music performed by recitalists, by opera companies and in symphonic concerts had the largest audiences they would ever have. Audiences knew and liked what they understood. At first it was a Wagnerian period, with many composers emulated his thick harmonies and extreme emotion. Later on the French Harmony of Debussy and Ravel prevailed amid mostly Beethoven and Mozart scores. Sprinkled in were occasional fashion pieces that tickled the ear with tolerable newness. Still, most music students, whether they wanted it or not, were exposed only to Traditional Theory. Increasingly in the 1930s, Radio broadcasts were added to the picture, thus solidifying the favorites listed above. Popular music also proliferated and began its journey, eventually monopolizing Radio and other emerging media. Then, after WWII, and while Traditional Theory remained in the classrooms, the tonal revolution roared back to life, this time with little hindrance.

In the 1920s, after the disruption WWI, when traditional music was limping back into being, along with the proliferating popular music aided by phonograph recordings, Arnold Schoenberg came upon a new system of handling pitches. He had not given up on his notion of atonal music. General audiences were seen as hindrances, minimal audiences were seen as honorable, as was marginalization. To hell with the common listener! This time a system was hit upon that rotated all 12 pitches equally. While Schoenberg was not the first to contemplate such a rotation, he was the first to refine the process so as to make each new composition linearly specific. His would be 12-Tone procedure that claimed a single chosen row (or serial) would automatically unify a piece or larger work. It was a method flexible enough to accommodate various types of composers, and to suit their particular notion of pitch-information feeding. It could even accommodate composers who preferred thirds and triads.

Here was a new approach to composition that could conceivably be classroom friendly, if only more teachers knew its rules. This serial approach to highly chromatic, (really duodecuple) music would only become famous by word of mouth. For decades few knew its procedures. The word of mouth also led to high-grade skepticism. And just maybe it promised more than it could deliver. Perhaps the resulting music gave rise to more intellectual interest in the process than in the actual music. This system could seemingly be taught to the few who showed interest, or who would desire to merely describe it. Particulars: The row itself would be a substitute for a tonic point of reference, and pitch or rhythmic motives could be incorporated in the scores. Also, to be a 12 Tone composer seemed for a while within easy grasp to those desiring quick fame. However, it would take decades before the realization that successful 12 Tone works involved a composer hearing his or her musical gestures independent of the process of assigning pitches dictated by the row. Certain objective techniques would fit into a classroom situation. Particularly friendly were 12 Tone works that simulated, or approximated the old Tonal ways.

AN OVERRIDING VIEW OF RHYTHM

The new modern music forced the need for defining and categorizing rhythm. After all, new rhythms were as indicative of the new era as were the handling of pitches. The following is a prospective on the use of rhythms throughout history.

A proposed definition of Rhythm: It is man's response to all perceived visual and aural experience, and his involuntary need to measure it in equal small units.

FOUR STAGES OF RHYTHM: Into which all composition ongoing rhythms fit.

First Stage: The listener can perceive the meter, and the grouping of measures into quadratic groupings. Classic and Romantic Period music present this most of the time.

Second Stage: The listener can perceive the meter, but not any easily grasped pattern of measure groupings. Most early historic, Baroque, and conservative 20th Century music present this.

Third Stage: The listener can perceive regular beats, but not any detectable meter. Some 20th Century music presents this.

Fourth Stage: The listener can perceive no beat regularity, though often beats can be easily seen on the written page.

A possible Fifth Stage rhythm: The listener is unaware of systematized tempo changes. (Tempo modulation) Pitch change, as well as note attacks, can be a primary tool for creating a particular stage of rhythm. Compositions may change Stages within a piece.

PITCH EFFICIENCY   A new concept that came about in conjunction with 12 – Tone writing.

The notion of Pitch Efficiency is perhaps one of the most radical and reviled in the whole history of music. In industry, work efficiency is seen as the removal or reduction of redundant bodily or spatial movement. In music, pitch efficiency means to avoid doubling or repeating pitches in close proximity. In using a 12-tone row a composer could decide how close the finished music would be to the sound of diatonic/triadic/TONALITY music. This closeness was judged highly inefficient, as well as laden with too much redolence of the past. Whereas Alban Berg produced a serial music that at times sounds deliberately close to diatonic melodies and tertian-structured chords (and hence appealing to a wider audience), his friend Anton Webern went the complete opposite in creating a music far removed from any such sounds. There arose in others a notion that the listener should be confronted with the effect of constantly new pitches. The listener, it was reasoned, would then be forced to pay attention to something more important.

We know there are only twelve pitches, but could they be presented in economical patterns? A listener would not hear any single pitch favored as an anchor, but is "cut free" to attend to other intended patterns. This way of thinking, as demonstrated by Webern, led to that abstraction: the precious score, or piece – lasting only a few minutes in length. To a limited constituency of listeners, such music coming Webern seemed natural. But later, with many deliberately imitative composers, the limited audience for such music would insure failure. If Rameau's suggestion, that the human ear hears diatonically is right, Pitch Efficiency would appear to be intended for listeners who do not exist. So it would seem that, among composers of the late 1900s, there would be a gradual awakening to the listener as performer. The majority of listeners can only process pitch and rhythmic information to a limited degree, and any new concept of composition must take that into account. An afterthought concerning Webern is that most of his many imitators failed to notice his attempts to create a new repertory of chords and progressions.

SCHENKER

During the first half of the 20th Century the writings of Heinrich Schenker and his students became somewhat widely known. (The writings of his student/interpreters were easily more accessible.) His methods dealt with how people can, or actually should hear music of the Classic and Romantic eras. He demonstrated rhythmically static graph-reductions of famous pieces and how the tonic and subsidiary chords and pitches are heard. His graphs involve ordinary notes and some unique symbols that demonstrate a hierarchy of tones and harmony, and how trained listeners actually hear, or memorize famous pieces. While the graphs can sometimes indicate basic motives, the primary thrust is in indicating harmonic stability amid temporary prolongation of subsidiary chords and tones. Schenker brought about the notion that a single melody can be plotted and heard in layers, in that a melody can rise to, or reach down to eventually resolve notes by step in each of the simultaneous layers. He made us conscious of Middle Ground harmony: Non-successive chords that are the pillars of the phrase. Whereas Schenker thought in more generalized concepts, his followers devised labels for different types of prolongation. Schenker further emphasized that, in a composition, there is only one tonic chord, regardless of various modulations. This last point would compromise Traditional Theory instruction that featured a new Roman numeral I applied to temporary modulations. (Remember that Rameau thought in tiny units with temporary tonics.) However, this minor disagreement with Schenker's fixed tonic principle, would not prevent convergence of Traditional Theory instruction with his principles.

Another noteworthy Schenker-related development late in the 20th Century was that certain composers of highly dissonant works wondered how a "middle ground" could be incorporated into their own works. However, and despite some efforts to "graph" 20th Century dissonant works, Schenkerian analysis would only remain voluble with music of the tonal era. Schenker's critics justifiably pointed out several weaknesses in the method: The graphs show little or nothing about rhythmic activity, nor the formal growth in a piece. Furthermore, two experts might graph the same piece somewhat differently. However, there are positive benefits in being able to reduce seemingly complex and unorganized pieces or groups of pieces into such compact illustrations. Groups of reductions can show similarity in whole bodies of works, that in turn, help to form conclusions about entire styles and repertories. For while there are infinite numbers of FOREGROUNDS, there are far fewer MIDDLEGROUNDs, and in tonal works only one BACKGROUND. The "Background" would be the tonic chord, enhanced by its penultimate V. Eventually, "Schenker" as a subject found its way into many Theory classrooms and textbooks after WW II. It certainly served as a convenient higher-level subject in advanced and graduate Theory courses. But adoption could also have a negative effect.

A curious development in the years after 1960, was that, since High Schools were improving their teaching of Traditional Theory, some students were showing up at their Freshman College Theory Classes knowing what had always been taught there. The result was that a few of the more prestigious Music Schools decided to teach only Schenkerian Theory to all levels in their basic courses. Traditional Theory had been mistakenly deemed a preparatory subject, unbefitting College level Theory instruction. However, that is a debatable conclusion. While Shenkerian instruction teaches students how they should be properly hear Tonal music, it can easily shortchange the students in many of the older traditional Theory instruction methods and their benefits. Perhaps a better approach is to blend basic Shenkerian concepts with Traditional SATB instruction, so as to more adequately prepare the student for a later Shenkerian focus.

HINDEMITH AS THEORIST

Schenker's highly persuasive methods were partially adapted by composer Paul Hindemith in his l930s book, dealing with Composition. Hindemith himself was going through a process of change as he entered the 1930s. He decided that dissonance, as well as an arbitrary personalized ways of composing were getting out of hand. So he took time out from composing to create his textbook (THE CRAFT OF COMPOSITION). While he still embraced the usage of all twelve tones in composing, they should be used so as to complement the tonic. He stressed the need for tension and release in using dissonance. In essence, he created an organized method of Neo-tonality. While all twelve tones could be used as a sort of pallet, some tones were more important than others, especially in establishing a tonic through the use of Perfect 5ths. He categorized chords according to their interval content, and demonstrated a scale of tension in their use. Some teachers and students were glad to compose in this sensible way, and the results were certainly more acceptable to a wider audience. But, by the closing decades of the 20th, Hindemith's method had become passé. Some critics even claimed that his students all sounded too alike in a new bogus Hindemith sound.

But some of Hindemith's Theoretical ideas bear rethinking. He spoke of harmony as a vital component in Composition, at a time when self-styled composers were "buying" into the curious notion that harmony either did not matter, that it should be solely the accident of simultaneous lines, or that it should be so deliberately anti-triadic that it would be startlingly new. (Such believers were convinced that from their day forward, all listeners would be listening linearly, and not for harmony.) For composers who did rely on the newly widened assortment of chords, Hindemith raised awareness of chords with, or without tritones in them. He also claimed that new chords, especially the non-triadic ones, could never be in chordal inversions. Therefore the only possible chordal Root is the lowest sounding the bass note.

PROGRESS IN PLOTTING/ANALYZING MELODIC LINES IN TONAL MUSIC

As far as classroom and private instruction were concerned, progress was made in objectifying how good melodies and lines were created through the writings and teachings of Schenker and Hindemith. Both would advocate what Schenker called prolongation methods, and that good lines "tonicized" certain notes by the use of nearby notes acoustically (Rameau) strong intervals. Though attention in Theory and Compositional instruction would remain understandably focused on chords and progressions, melodies and lines would now have some method for discussion and analysis.

A NEW APPROACH TO THEORY INSTRUCTION and its apparent failure.

Another development stemming from the Hindemith Composition book was an attempt to redefine what Theory instruction should be. In the l940s one of Hindemith's outstanding students, Bernhard Heiden, began teaching Composition at Indiana University. Evidently he motivated some of his students there to create Basic Theory texts that treated Theory as if it were solely a method to learn how to compose. Armed with good intentions that far exceeded the results, Hindemith's whole method of looking at tonal music was extended by examining repertory from the past and present, and explaining it using the newer terms and concepts. For a couple of mid-century 1900s decades, music students at Indiana University were trained in this new, and some felt, curious thinking and terminology. (At the time the Indiana University Music School was the largest in the nation, and had an enormous number of enrolled instrumentalists.) All of music, as well as Theory instruction were promoted as a study in linear process, reinforcing a tonic. Much of the Traditional Theory gains and methods were either minimized or ignored entirely. Undergraduate students, primarily oriented to instrumental performance, easily adapted to the new approach. If they had any previous Theory, it involved the basics of the old method, and were convinced it was passé. Many Graduate assistants from other schools, having been trained in more Traditional methods, struggled to assimilate what they had learned earlier with the new, and some would say, courageous Theory methods. However, this approach had to ignore and avoid too many of the solid gains that Traditional Theory had achieved in unlocking the inner mechanics of the standard repertory. So inevitably, the Hindemith/Heiden influenced texts would be abandoned late in the 20th century.

Another development that weakened Theory instruction was the so-called Comprehensive Music efforts, beginning in the 1960s. Well-meaning reformers had determined that Music Theory was doing a poor job of showing how its instruction linked into the greater music picture. The solution was that all higher-level instruction should "cross-blend." Music Theory, Music History, performance practice should be blended in to whatever the course of instruction was supposed to be about. Obviously if brought about, this approach would end up watering down specific subject instruction. It also denied that students, at least the ones headed for success, had any ability to cross-fertilize discrete subjects. This wrong-headed approach also seemed to confuse in many instructors' minds as to just what Theory is. It is a fact that the 1960s saw an increase in iconoclasm, with many of its exponents out to prove that most old methods were bad. There appeared many individuals who had all the latest, supposedly improved methods of instruction. It may be that the Comprehensive Music approach died a quiet, well-deserved death.

12 TONE INSTRUCTION
In the early 1940s a tiny pamphlet created by composer Ernst Krenek was published in the U. S. Krenek had been a refugee from Hitler's Europe, and he would have a long and successful teaching career in the U.S.A. In his pamphlet-size book Krenek proceeded to explain the 12-Tone method innovated in the early 1920s by Arnold Schoenberg. (He never studied with him.) As far as the English speaking world was concerned, this was the first textbook on the subject. Among the usual explanations of the row and its four versions, Krenek attempted to show how the rotation of 12 different pitches was not as unmusical as uninformed followers and critics had claimed. Krenek pointed out that the strict rules in creating the row as were being confused with the freer approaches in using the row to compose. He demonstrated methods of slowing down pitch information through row portion repetitions. After the end of WWII there would be a profusion of 12-Tone books and spokesmen who followed Krenek's lead. There would be much dodecaphonic analyzing and composing in most Music departments and schools. Eventually there would be at least three numerical methods of analyzing row usage: 1. Ordinal, 2.) Assigning fixed numbers to specific pitch classes, and 3.) Interval class usage (Six intervals: 1 through 6). In time this led to dissatisfaction. "Row-counting" seemed to prove little because it failed to deal with what was felt to be the essential musicality and formal structure in a score. It was how the composer used the row that mattered, and that element proved more elusive.

THE USE OF NUMBERS – AGAIN
Throughout the 1900s a few notable figures advocated a reliance on numerical systems, either as an aid, or for actual compositional ideation. This seems to be a throwback to the Classic Greek days when Pythagoras and others saw numbers and music being inseparable. In the post WWI years Joseph Schillinger devised an approach to the Arts using mathematics. (Eventually two somewhat heavy volumes were published in 1949.) Good music, as he saw it, could be calculated. Though his most famous private student was George Gershwin, there is no proof that Gershwin ever used his ideas. The Schillinger system did not catch on.

It would not be long when Schoenberg's 12-tone method would be connected with mod 12 numbers, thus enabling mathematics in placing the four forms of the same row put into a so-called Magic Square. This would assist in analysis of 12-tone works, but only in terms of row tracings, never composing. Schoenberg himself advised that in the creation of music the duodecuple ideation should come first in the opening measures, after which row information should be extracted in order to proceed. Put another way, music linear ideation should be the master of row pitch use, not the other way around. One hears a melodic contour, then one assigns pitches from the row to bring about that contour. Nonetheless, 12-tone Theory could be classroom-friendly.

In time it would become obvious that in analyzing a piece by merely row-trace revealed very little about the musical process or form of a well-composed piece. But times change. From 1945 to 2000, as theoretical tools improved for "row-counting," serial 12-tone music itself fell into disfavor. It would be in the province of Theorists to deal with all aspects of successful works from the past that used this 12-tone technique, and any numerical aid in analysis.

Set Theory and Interval Vectors seemingly came about at the same time. Both were analytical approaches that appear handier in analyzing note usage in atonal (as opposed to 12-Tone) pieces, though other adapted uses are possible. While Set Theory can use numbers up to and including 11, the Vector system limits interval sizes to only six. The tritone is the largest and is assigned a "6" because of its six half-steps. In the case of Set Theory usually small motives (Sets) are assigned numbers, with the first note being assigned a "0." For instance 0156. Here the order of the pitches does not matter. That is an important break-through in analysis. It would also be possible to think of the set as a (seemingly radical) "harmony" that could be transposed and used throughout a piece. Set Theory, as an analytical tool, helped analyzers to connect with certain composers' minds involving hitherto enigmatic pieces. Interval Vectors, on the other hand, would prove to be a limited analytical tool. Restricting itself to mod 0 through 6 size intervals, they would enable one to measure the interval content of a 12-Tone Row, any Set, or even Tonal chords and scales. This would shed further light on analysis of works. But, aside from statistical relationships, how important is that light? Another glaring weakness of Vectors is the difficulty of transferring back and forth from notes on staves to Vectors. Hitherto, all use of numerical symbols easily transferred back and forth.

In the 1950s massively sized computers began coming about, and early on there would be a composer who found a special way to use this new capability. Iannis Xenokis, a Greek ex-patriot, who originally created some seminal Electronic works, was interested in "clouds" of random sounds. He would spend the l960s and '70s creating works for orchestra that would be in traditional notation, but were calculated from the random pitch and rhythmic patterns created by his "Stocastic" computer program. In the creation of the scores, he was still in charge of writing down the notes to be read by symphonic players, but he sought out and reveled in the effect created by what he called "clouds" of sounds. He likened the sound-clouds to a forest of newly awakened cicadas.

By the end of the 1900s, as computer technology became more expensively advanced, there would be a number of research centers that welcomed studies in computer assistance and possible music creation, music copying and score creation, artificial intelligence, and all manner of musical connections. Predictably there would be occasional "stunts" that demonstrated a computer composing on its own. However, it would seem that, so far, and other than small pockets of novelty enthusiasts, there has been no distinguishable effect on the on-going continuum of human written music ideation and its positive perception by audiences. If anything, there seems to have been a decisive reaction by the majority against a technology gone awry.

NON MELODIC LINE MUSIC
Sometime in the years after WWII, a constituency desiring to promote a new modern music, decided that lines and melodies were but one parameter to exploit in composition. Now music, it was felt, would get close to mathematics by using a Mathematical label and concept that opened the door for scores that demonstrated other musical ingredients that were not melodic. Among some in this constituency, any scores that relied on melody and lines, to say nothing about harmony, were deemed out of touch and old-fashioned. Other parameters could be rhythm, timbre, and any other measurable feature of acoustical music.

NEW NOTATIONAL SYMBOLS
It was probably in the 1960s when there were attempts to create book-compendiums of various new notation symbols, both for instrumental and choral music. After WWII various European, and later American composers began inventing symbols to indicate new sounds and decorations made possible on acoustical instruments. Performers were being confronted with a written language that was at first foreign. The wise composer included in the score a legend that explained what each symbol meant. A problem was that various composers used their own symbols for the same sound or special effect. The compendiums that were published in the 1960s were attempts at standardization. As decades passed, however, the bulk of the symbols and their various effects seemed to pass into history. And moreover, maybe most of the innovations and scores of the

"revolutionary" 1960s, as well, became passé. This does not, however, rule out any future resurgence of interest.

SPECULATIVE WRITINGS IN THE JOURNALS

New perceptions on Theory and Composition would remain as part of the Theory picture. 20th Century journals continued that tradition. As was said earlier, determined Theorists and teachers of the subject, remained and will remain avid readers of new suppositions or analyses. Occasionally there is such an interest, that it did not, nor does not matter if the new conceptions ever led to positive change. What matters is that the brain cells are stimulated by excitement or novelty of reading about new concepts.

MORE PROBLEMS FOR THE THEORY CLASS

For a while in the late 20th Century it seemed as if there was an attempt by some university thinkers to separate Theory from Composition, so as to make Theory independent in itself. It would have its own essay writers, way of thinking, vocabulary, pretense of being a mock-science, hierarchy (pecking order) of the writers, value system, and success awards. To a certain extent, Theory instruction in higher education should certainly be separated from creative composition courses. However, Theory, considering its timeless role of "chasing" compositional practices in search of answers, will always be supplemental to Composition. Any attempts above that station will be met with marginalization and eventual redundancy.

Classroom Theory instruction, indeed any Theory pedagogy is dependent on showing how an entire body of work is based on discernable notation and formal patterns, and in turn how those patterns are influential over time. However, what if the method of score creation is based on uniqueness of each work, upon anti-pattern thinking, or upon the sense that through excessive repetition, change is calculated to be in the listener's mind, rather than in the music heard? This all negates the function of the Theory classroom. Already beginning in the 1920s, it seemed that Theorist/Teachers were forever chasing the latest composition techniques in attempts to explain them in classrooms. At that time it was the newly emerging 12-tone method. Its very premise promised possible classroom use. However, for the time being there would be very few musical examples, and a developing World War that would interrupt any progress. After war's end in 1945 much progress would be made in passing along the Theory-friendly 12 –tone procedures. But then during that same period, the 12-tone method was already passé and taking a back seat to other compositional developments and outright compositional upheavals. The post-war years were a time of intense individualism in the Arts. The accepted thinking was that such and such a score or composer was unique in personage and in product. Teachers resorted to merely citing people and scores, and describing methods in general terms.

Some innovations could be described as non-teachable. For instance, whatever John Cage did could never be explained in Theoretical terms, nor could it be taught to students. The John Cage message says to all that they should be uniquely themselves. However, that is easier said than done. Apparently Cage's remarkable pieces began with a unique non-musical glimmer in his mind that usually had nothing to do with combining notes on a page. Such unique glimmers are not teachable, other than for "surfacy" discussion in the classroom. Moreover, it is akin to saying that any fiction author should invent their own letters, words and concepts, so as to reveal themselves as being unique (as well as impenetrable). Thus communication with most others is seriously hampered, if not prevented. Such thinking, other than for mere mentioning, will not work in classroom instruction.

Another reality, and probably the result of Cage-like thinking, is the distrust of the human mind to conjure up new compositions because of remembering of all the heard music of the past. Such reasoning is based on a few myths. The first is that composition must be totally and starkly original. However, that is not the way music happened throughout history. In the past every time a dominant composer came along, there is evidence that he or she were combining the old with their concept of the new. So, while we can appreciate individuals wanting to utilize systems, technology, multi-parameter serialization, or whatever, we had better reason that they were/are really searching for new sound concepts. There would still be the problem of weaving those new sounds into listenable music? Some people in the 20th Century held onto the myth that so long as a sonic experience is starkly new it is, or would eventually lead to esthetic experience in the listener.

Sonic concepts found at the "back of beyond" might easily result in scores no one wants to hear. (And maybe stark originality at any price is more about the originator than the score. "Are you pushing yourself, or your music?") Ultimately a new range of sounds should be part of combining the old with the new, and, above all, communicating with a targeted audience. Seen in that light, the entire movement, aside from a few masterpieces, is really part of the ongoing search for new useful sounds that will ultimately end up transferred to standard musical instrumentation. Also, seen in that light, the finished products of the so-called multi-parameter serialists, active in Darmstadt, Germany immediately after WWII then make sense. This reasoning was certainly behind Xenokis's computer-generated stochastic programs. First get the sounds, then musically put them into scores.

As has been pointed out, the intense search by certain composers for originality at any price during the immediate post WWII decades has certainly created instruction problems for the classroom? Certainly while the too-totally-unique has a dubious place in the world of Composition, and apart from mere citation purposes, it most certainly has no place in the world of private or classroom Theory instruction. How could it be?

ANALOG and DIGITAL ELECTRONIC MUSIC
Not much will be said about this area, even though its instruction seemed/seems to fall under the aegis of Theory, almost by default. While the history of this post WWII movement is fascinating, all concerns with these media lie outside the scope of this book. The sounds of these media do not involve sufficient commitment to paper. Rather, the ideation involves working and manipulating the sounds themselves. Interest in electronically produced sounds, while initially high in the 1950s and '60s, has waned. By the start of the 21st Century the entire movement seemed to have been reduced to near cult-status. Aside from small pockets of followers, would any significantly lasting repertory come about? And would that repertory be forever locked in its original recording? (Unlike classic repertory that lives again and again through new performances.) Was it all a passing fad, doomed to be taken up by technology quidnuncs who have no interest in classic music treasures of the past? Also, music student interest in the various gadgets and indeed in technology itself, seemed to largely disappear by 2000. The Electronic music movement, moreover, raised many questions concerning its place in the training of music students. Did the students need to know all the technicalities of frequency and amplitude modulation, filtering, envelopes, etc.? Were the facilities, upkeep, and necessary help-engineers all too expensive for limited budgets in the face of so few interested individuals? Also, there remains a collision of incompatible values. The manufacturers of technological equipment are profit-minded concerns that often could, did, and will continue to eliminate old products after they have earned a profit. Contrast that with the mind set of musicians over the centuries who stayed with the piano or violin permanently. Maybe Technological music belongs in the realm of private instruction outside of institutions.

MUSICAL DISSONANCE AS AN AREA FOR UNIVERSITY RESEARCH
During the so-called Modern Music period, now perhaps identified as 1945 to 1965, and incongruous as it sounds, some universities and other institutions were funding, and seeking foundation grants to study (extreme?) dissonance in music. This was a reaction to musical scores that had appeared that had pushed dissonance, as well as other "parameters," to the extreme. This was probably in keeping with composers who were competing with one another to produce unique "sound experiences" of the most radical type. While some involved with this were more attracted to Science, than to music., others were interested in self-promotion. Mixed in with this was the Electronic Music medium, its advocates, composers and limited audience. (A sympathetic view of the analog electronic music can easily be made, and some gains were made in the growth of music.) Just how this debatable "research" venture turned out is still a mystery because there seems to have been no measurable effect on the ongoing history of composition. However, for a while the Grant-recipients were riding

high, and the universities involved were at last enabled to assist in the sustenance of an imagined "Higher Art."

OTHER 20TH CENTURY PROBLEMS:
The 20th Century began, and just before WWI, a New Music movement began and was, no doubt, led by individuals who believed in linear growth in the Arts. But just what is "growth" in music, or the Arts? It is probably something vastly subtler than well-meaning extremists sought. Compare the traditional music with the most radical scores of 1912-13. If there is Arts growth, it is linear and not exponential. If the 20th Century deserved the "new," just how new should it be? Allowing for the occasional unique masterpiece, how far should innovation go? How much of the potential audience can be ignored? How much are composers justified in claiming that their music is aimed at future audiences, and how far into the future? As said above, musical growth is probably something vastly subtler than the extremists would have it.

There were inevitable limits to a "competition to shock," which peaked in the 1960s,and a spontaneous reaction set in beginning in the 1970s. Questions were asked: Just what is music? Just who comprises the audience? Who are these people who seem to be leading us astray? What was music before all this upheaval began? What and who will benefit from studies in dissonance? Is the audience for Art Music going to dwindle to nothing? Are machines creating music for other machines? How do humans listen to music? Is there no end to artistic revolution succeeding artistic revolution? Is there not some compromise in adding new techniques to ordinary music that is not intended to merely publicize individuals? But, no matter what chaotic developments had taken place on concert stages and on recordings throughout that Modern Period, Traditional Music Theory instruction continued privately and in classrooms.

Also by the end of the 20th Century a new problem arose: The process of introducing new compositions was hindered by the "one-time experience,"-existentialist frame-of-mind. Score-preparers and small audiences were sold on the idea that hearing a new work was an enjoyable experience locked in the immediate moment. "Why hear a score again? I had that unusual experience already, and have no need to experience it again." Well, this leads to an entirely new ball game, and obviously to "throwaway scores" galore. All of the above problems were somewhat solved, or ameliorated by the ability to replay music via recordings. Valuable music was more easily identified through repeated hearings, as were the incomprehensible, overly cerebrally created note combinations. In the 1920s Ravel commented on an influx of "intellectual" scores. The Ravel comment suggests that true music comes from a certain part of the brain, and not the rational part. Many writers on Esthetics would agree.

Considering Composition and Theory instruction:

A few open-ended basic questions were raised in the 20th Century, the answers of which would affect the kind of music composers would then, and will create. Here are a few of them:

What happens in the brain of the targeted listener when he or she is confronted with

1.) Absolute newness in the form of tidbits stated only once, or a texture that is overwhelmingly thick, resulting in a tonal continuum that remains irrelevant even after repeated hearings?

    Are the majority of good-faith listeners unalterably limited by a hearing mechanism that is by nature diatonic?

2.) The seemingly endless repetition of small musical tidbits in so-called minimalistic music?

        Is it a valid music experience when the listener is lulled into a mesmeric state?

The above questions deal with musical information feeding, and the taking into account of how listeners process musical information.

As the 2000s begin, the progress in of written music ideation, and the imparting of higher-level artistic sensitivity, are threatened by the over-prevalence and seeming triumph of popular music. It would seem that most humans can, and are being conditioned by mass media to support music of a vastly simple nature. This, of course, leads to an endless cycle of self-renewing simple-mindedness. It is also a form of bondage, preventing or delaying potential mental growth in one of life's pleasures. It would seem that the human being has a right to grow, and anything impeding that right is inherently wrong.

POSTSCRIPT:

It is hoped that this is the correct approach to the subject, and that any deficiencies in this book can be corrected and improved by future writers.

Bibliography

Shirlaw, Matthew, The Theory of Harmony, London: Novello & Co., 1917
Randel, Don Michael, The New Harvard Dictionary of Music, Harvard U. Press, 1986
Apel, Willi, Harvard Dictionary of Music, Harvard U. Press, 1969
Riemann, Hugo, History of Music Theory, reprint Da Capo Press 1974
Grout , Donald Jay, A History of Western Music, W. W. Norton, Inc., 1960 edition